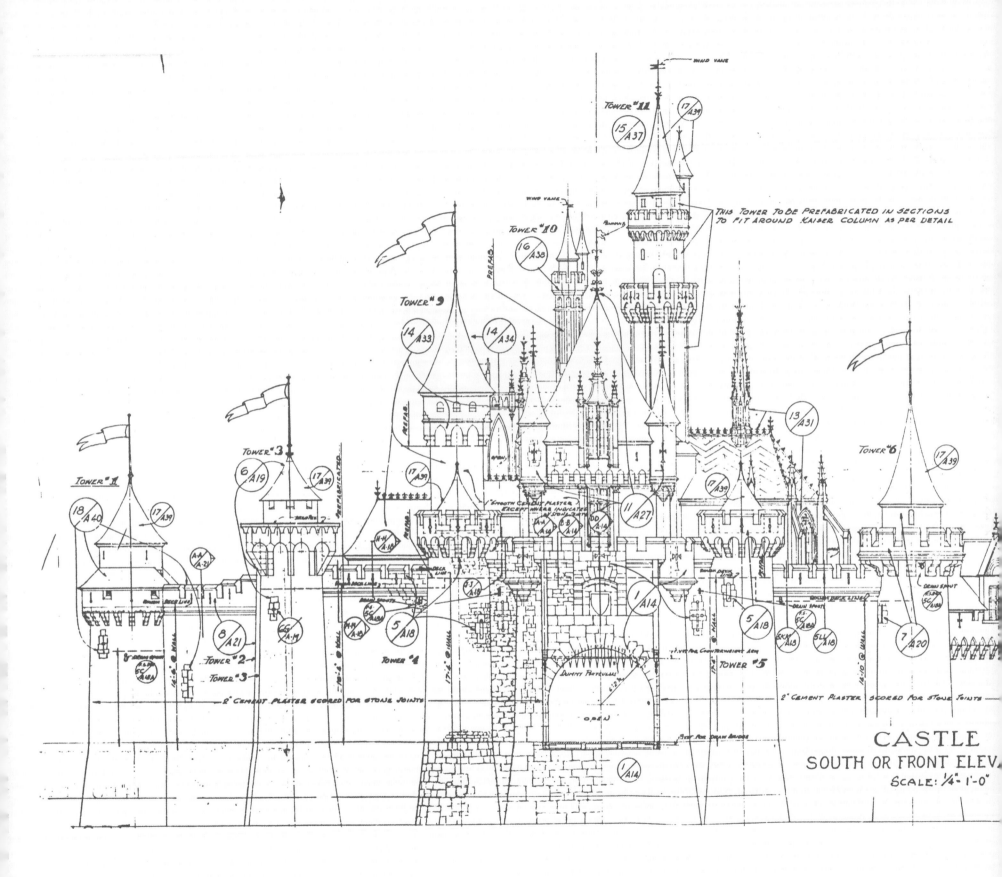

CASTLE
SOUTH OR FRONT ELEV.
SCALE: 1/4" = 1'-0"

DISNEYLAND
THROUGH THE DECADES
A Photographic Celebration

By Jeff Kurtti

Foreword by Marty Sklar

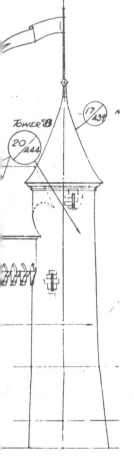

DISNEY EDITIONS

Disneyland Through the Decades:
A Photographic Celebration

For Disney Editions
Wendy Lefkon, Editorial Director
Pamela Bobowicz, Associate Editor
Jessica Ward, Assistant Editor
Jennifer Eastwood, Managing Editor

Designed by Impress, Inc.
Hans Teensma, Creative Director
James McDonald, Art Director
www.impressinc.com
Michael Carroll, Chief Photographer

Printed in the United States of America
First Edition
Jacketed Edition: ISBN 978-1-4231-2905-9
Slipcase Edition: ISBN 978-1-4231-2904-2
F322-8368-0-10032
Library of Congress Catalog Card Number on file
Visit www.disneybooks.com

PHOTO RIGHT: *Peter Ellenshaw works on his iconic painting of* Disneyland *Park, 1954.*

INTRODUCTION

The story of *Disneyland* Park has been told time and again, and in many different forms: as earnest history, architectural review, sprightly souvenir, postcard chronicle, comic book, hagiography, biographical representation, cultural summary, or treatise of the sinister transformation of innocuous American popular culture into malevolent capitalist playground.

It is a subject that has fascinated since its inception, and continues to fascinate to this day. Since that sweltering Sunday in July 1955 when Walt Disney dedicated his new park to "the ideals, the dreams, and the hard facts that have created America ... with the hope that it will be a source of joy and inspiration to all the world," *Disneyland* Park has welcomed more than 500 million visitors from around the world, and continues to introduce new forms of entertainment and technology that fulfill Walt Disney's vision that "Disneyland will never be completed. It will continue to grow as long as there is imagination left in the world."

Counted among the greatest entertainment achievements of the twentieth century, *Disneyland* Park introduced an entirely new concept in family entertainment and launched today's global theme park industry. In creating *Disneyland* Park, Walt Disney sparked the world's imagination and established an international icon—a beloved, vibrant, and relevant landmark on the pop culture landscape. Its success and renown have paved the way for the ten Disney parks around the world that have followed its innovative model.

Disneyland Park itself has grown over the years to become a 510-acre, multi-faceted, world-class family resort destination, complete with three award-winning hotels, two celebrated Disney theme parks, and a stimulating shopping, dining, and entertainment area called *Downtown Disney* District.

Today, more than six generations of families and friends from across the United States and around the world have grown up with the familiar and comforting experience of *Disneyland* Resort, making it a treasured part of the collective consciousness.

In approaching the creation of another book about *Disneyland* Resort, I sought the advice of someone who knows it pretty well: a fifty-four-year Disney employee and the recently retired

◀◀ A "great big beautiful tomorrow" was the optimistic futurism that greeted *Disneyland* Park visitors beginning in 1967; a bright, gleaming, kinetic future where technology promised freedom.

The problem with ▶▶ "tomorrow" is that by today it becomes yesterday. *Tomorrowland* Area has evolved into a celebration of imagined futures: yesterday's tomorrow today.

Walt Disney Imagineering Ambassador, Marty Sklar. Marty has a little experience in this field, having written the first book about *Disneyland* Park back in 1965, and contributing to pretty much every single book on the subject since then. He made a few key connections for me that really informed this volume:

He suggested that yet another "History of *Disneyland* Resort" was more than a bit super-fluous. He reminded me to create a work that is not just for the dyed-in-the-wool Disney fan, but one that would captivate and engage a generation of new Disney enthusiasts. ("Not everyone has every Disneyland book ever printed lined up on their bookshelf like you do, Jeff.")

He suggested a work that touches the heart and the mind, combining a primarily visual celebration with thoughtful writing.

So, this book is a little different in the library of works about *Disneyland* Resort. But in a way it hearkens to the books about *Disneyland* Park that I had when I was a child, when what was left unsaid or unexplained stimulated curiosity and imagination; and I would look for what seemed like hours at the same photo, until I had observed and absorbed every infinitesimal detail—a surrogate experience for my ability to escape Seattle and go to the actual *Disneyland* Park!

Disneyland Resort is one of the most-photographed locations on earth for a reason: pictures of the resort are not only charming and beautiful; they tell evocative stories, call to mind memories, and create a genuine longing to visit the actual place—and enjoy the real experience.

Within these pages is a celebration of timelessness. Many of the images contained here evoke the past, but in doing so, celebrate the enduring currency and relevance of *Disneyland* Resort.

—Jeff Kurtti
Glendale, California
June 2009

FOREWORD

Marty Sklar,
former Walt Disney
Imagineering
Ambassador,
on *Main Street,
U.S.A.* Area.

On the tenth anniversary of *Disneyland* Park, in 1965, Walt and Roy O. Disney assembled the leaders of the *Disneyland* Park operating team, and the key designers of WED Enterprises (now Walt Disney Imagineering) and set in motion their future: "If any of you thinks we can rest on our laurels, forget it! We're just getting started!"

Walt Disney's "marching orders" were nothing new to the assembled *Disneyland* cast members and Imagineers. When he was asked on Opening Day, July 17, 1955, when *Disneyland* Park would be finished (because so much was "barely done" or "not quite ready"), Walt's reply was a classic that has echoed down the pages of time: "Disneyland will never be completed," he promised, "as long as there is imagination left in the world."

Promise made, promise kept. Almost every year since 1955, *Disneyland* Park has added something new and often revolutionary and trend-setting in the attraction industry: the first attractions capable of carrying over 3,000 guests per hour (*it's a small world* Attraction and *Pirates of the Caribbean* Attraction); new storytelling systems like *Audio-Animatronics* Figures that "brought to life" birds in *The Enchanted Tiki Room*, and President Abraham Lincoln in *Great Moments With Mr. Lincoln* to remind Guests about America's liberties and values; unique storytelling in parades and fireworks shows that light up the skies every night; and more fun in transportation aboard trains, monorails, submarines, jungle boats, and Autopia cars (for many a youngster, their first time at the controls of a "real" auto), trips to outer space and, in an early version, *inner space*, a journey through "The Might Microscope," now gone but not forgotten. And so much more.

I met Walt Disney for the first time two weeks before *Disneyland* Park opened. As the editor of my college newspaper, the *Daily Bruin* at UCLA, I had been hired to write and edit a tabloid newspaper, 1890s style, to be sold for ten cents on *Main Street, U.S.A.* Area. After two weeks on the job, I had to present the concept and early drafts to Walt Disney himself. Fortunately, he liked it—and thus began my own fifty-four-year career at Disney, ten of them writing material for Walt for *Disneyland* Park souvenir guides, presentations to potential sponsors, narrations for the Disney shows at the New York World's Fair of 1964–65, and even a film introducing his concepts for *Walt Disney World* Resort, and a community Walt called EPCOT. What continually amazed me, from that very first meeting in the midst of the construction chaos around us, was his focus on even the smallest detail. My little twenty-eight-page newspaper did not mean much in the overall picture of the birth of *Disneyland* Park, except—it was a story point for Walt Disney, the recognized great storyteller. After all, every small town in the era of the Park's *Main Street, U.S.A.* Area, 1890–1910, had its own newspaper. Could the Park really be true to the times without that tabloid? Not to the master storyteller, Walt Disney!

From the beginning, the public "got it." Beyond its business success, *Disneyland* Park proved to be a cultural triumph—perhaps even beyond the imagination of Walt himself. Immediately, "Disneyland" became pop shorthand for *the* destination in California, an affectionate goal for family travel, and an almost mystical objective of wonder for travelers from around the world—presaging the day when there would be sister Disney parks in Tokyo, Paris, Hong Kong, and across the U.S.A. in Orlando, Florida. Here was the collective culture of the Disney Studio's beloved storytelling, brought to life as a physical place, where each visitor became a part of the tale—and had the ability to translate that experience into their personal mythology.

Soon every Guest—adults, children, families, heads of state, celebrities—included *Disneyland* Park in their plans. Many people began incorporating *Disneyland* Park into their significant events and celebrations; before long, it was simply woven into the fabric of people's lives. Over the decades, *Disneyland* Park has become an adored anomaly: historic but ever changing, ever timely and yet timeless, a great public place and an intimate personal experience.

This book is a reflection of the *Disneyland* Resort in all the foregoing incarnations and identities, a visual celebration of not only art and architecture, but of the very individual experiences that have made *Disneyland* Park through the decades truly *"the happiest place on earth!"*

—*Marty Sklar*
December 2009

Walt decided that
the Rivers of America
needed more traffic,
and the construction
supervisor of
Disneyland Park
(and a former naval
admiral) Joe Fowler
recommended the
Columbia. Architect
Ray Wallace worked
with Fowler in
creating the plans;
the ship was con-
structed at Todd
Shipyards in San
Pedro, California.

IN LOVING MEMORY OF

Roy Edward Disney

1930–2009

He understood the power of the name
and its meaning to millions around the world.

DISNEYLAND THROUGH THE DECADES

1952–1955

Disneyland Dreams

"It came about when my daughters were very young and Saturday was always daddy's day with the two daughters," Walt Disney recalled in a 1963 interview. "…I'd take them to the merry-go-round and … sit on a bench, eating peanuts. I felt that there should be something built where the parents and the children could have fun together. So that's how Disneyland started."

That, then, became the *Disneyland* Park dogma. But Walt's recollection is only a component of the evolution of *Disneyland* Park, and it is as interesting for the elements it omits as for those it contains. Walt's demotion of the lengthy and complex intellectual and creative process was simply, "I started with many ideas, threw them away, started all over again. And eventually it evolved into what you see today at Disneyland."

Walt had always been a fan of the circus, carnivals, and fairs. His father, Elias, had been a laborer on The World's Columbian Exposition of 1893 in Chicago, and he must certainly have regaled his young son with tales of its wonders. Walt had created a custom Mickey Mouse cartoon for the 1939 New York World's Fair, and had been an enthusiastic visitor to the "other" 1939 Fair, The Golden Gate International Exposition in San Francisco.

Since boyhood, Walt was entranced by the power, romance, and the culture of railroading. As a boy, he had been a "news butcher," selling newspapers, peanuts, and candy on the railroad out of Kansas City. He attended, with animator Ward Kimball, the Chicago Railroad Fair in 1948, and the meticulous nostalgia of Henry Ford's Greenfield Village in Dearborn, Michigan. Soon after his return, he combined his miniature-making hobby with his love of trains and affection for Americana.

He began building a $1/8$-scale model of a Central Pacific Locomotive of the 1870s to circle his Holmby Hills property. Dubbed "The Carolwood Pacific," the train helped him escape the pressures of the Studio.

◀◀ Ever utilizing cutting-edge technology, Walt Disney departs from his Burbank Studio via helicopter. Destination: *Disneyland* Park!

Agriculture gives ▶▶
way to an entertain-
ment destination,
1954.

However burdensome it might have been for him at times, the Studio he had completed in Burbank in 1940 had been another unexpected creative blessing for Walt. He threw himself into every detail of its design and execution just as he had with his filmmaking endeavors. He was very proud of the results, and he contemplated offering Studio tours, but couldn't imagine anything more dull than watching people make movies—especially animated ones. Still, he kept receiving requests from kids who wanted to visit and see where Mickey Mouse and Snow White lived.

As early as 1940, animator Ben Sharpsteen recalled that Walt was thinking of creating displays of Disney characters in their fantasy surroundings on land adjacent to the Studio, so that visitors might see something more than "just people working." John Hench remembers looking out the window and seeing Walt in the distance, pacing off the wasted sliver of land between the Studio and the Los Angeles Flood Control Channel.

In the late 1940s, these concepts began to amalgamate as Walt began yet another, separate project, known variously as "Walt Disney's America" and "Disneylandia," which would tour department stores across the country, featuring dimensional animated miniature scenes of America's past, including a vaudeville hoofer and a barbershop quartet. This idea soon expanded to a custom railroad train with each car featuring the miniature shows and other evocations of American nostalgia.

Ideas coalesced. In 1948, Walt circulated a memo about his "kiddie park" idea with detailed descriptions of *Main Street, U.S.A.* Area and *Frontierland* Area. In 1952, Disney presented a plan for an amusement park to the city of Burbank for approval, this one containing elements of futurism and fantasy. By the summer of 1953, Walt had engaged the Stanford Research Institute to find a property of the right size and location to maximize this new project's creative and commercial potential.

Everything from his first visit to the circus as a child to his last trip around his backyard railroad had, at last, culminated in the undertaking that Walt would call "Disneyland."

So, what we know today as *Disneyland* Resort had a gestation of nearly half a century. For posterity, *Disneyland* Park was simply a "magical little park" that grew out of the desire of a weary father, with two young daughters in tow, who merely wanted "an amusement enterprise built where the parents and the children could have fun together." ■

A NEW CONCEPT IN FAMILY ENTERTAINMENT

Disneyland

Fant

FRONTIERLAND

A log fort, stage coaches, Indians, mule-pack trains, stern-wheeler riverboat and a pioneer street help to make Frontierland a living re-creation of America's past.

Adventureland

Devoted to natural wonders, Adventureland offers a cruise on an explorer's boat through tropical rivers of the world, past animated birds, beasts and reptiles.

AB 755

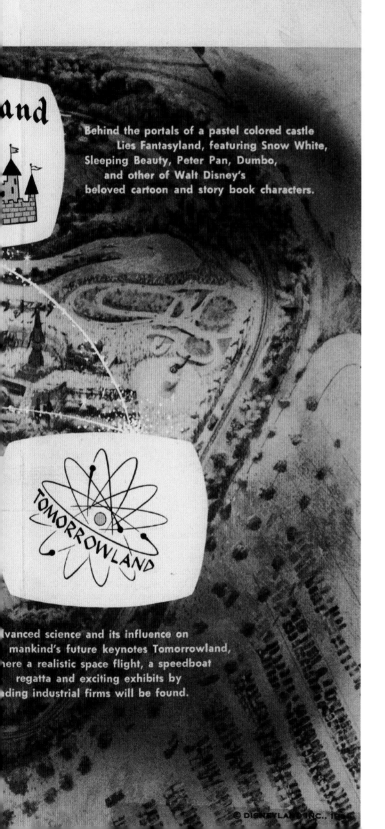

160 ACRES OF HAPPINESS IN ANAHEIM, CALIFORNIA

Behind the portals of a pastel colored castle
Lies Fantasyland, featuring Snow White,
Sleeping Beauty, Peter Pan, Dumbo,
and other of Walt Disney's
beloved cartoon and story book characters.

TOMORROWLAND

...vanced science and its influence on
    mankind's future keynotes Tomorrowland,
    ...here a realistic space flight, a speedboat
    regatta and exciting exhibits by
    ...ding industrial firms will be found.

Creative concepts
flowed like water
from Disney artists,
1953.

◄◄ Walt Disney
Productions' 1954
annual report trum-
pets the new notion
of *Disneyland* Park.

DISNEYLAND PARK PROPOSAL

Sometime—in 1955—will present for the people of the world—and to children of all ages—a new experience in entertainment.

In these pages is proffered a glimpse into this great adventure . . . a preview of what the visitor will find in Disneyland.

—Walt Disney

The Disneyland Story

The idea of Disneyland is a simple one. It will be a place for people to find happiness and knowledge.

It will be a place for parents and children to share pleasant times in one another's company: a place for teacher and pupils to discover greater ways of understanding and education. Here the older generation can recapture the nostalgia of days gone by, and the younger generation can savor the challenge of the future. Here will be the wonders of Nature and Man for all to see and understand.

Disneyland will be based upon and dedicated to the ideals, the dreams, and hard facts that have created America. And it will be uniquely equipped to dramatize these dreams and facts and

send them forth as a source of courage and inspiration to all the world.

Disneyland will be something of a fair, an exhibition, a playground, a community center, a museum of living facts, and a showplace of beauty and magic.

It will be filled with the accomplishments, the joys, and hopes of the world we live in. And it will remind us and show us how to make these wonders part of our own lives.

Inside Disneyland

Like Alice stepping through the looking glass, to step through the portals of Disneyland will be like entering another world. Within a few steps the visitor will find himself in a small mid-Western town at the turn of the century.

The Railroad Station, situated at the main entrance to Disneyland, is recommended as a starting point for the visitor. Here, you may board a $1/3$-scale train pulled by a twelve-ton steam engine, six feet high. At the start of Main Street is Civic Center, with its Town Hall, Fire Station, Police Station, and the old Opera House, which houses the broadcasting

theatre for the Walt Disney Television Show. From Civic Center you can take a horse-drawn streetcar up Main Street or hire a surrey and driver.

Main Street

Main Street has the nostalgic quality that makes it everybody's hometown. It is Main Street, U.S.A. Three blocks long, it is the main shopping district of Disneyland. It has a bank and a newspaper office, and the little ice cream parlor with the marble-topped tables and wire-backed chairs. There is a penny arcade and a Nickelodeon where you can see old-time movies.

On the corner is the great Disneyland Emporium where you can buy almost anything and everything unusual. Clothes, cowboy boots, toys, records, books, ceramics, old-fashioned candies, jaw-breakers, and licorice whips. Toys from all over the world. Gifts for the person who has "everything." Or you can get the big mail-order catalogue and purchase by mail.

You'll find quaint little restaurants on Main Street with family style cooking, and a bakery shop where Johnny can watch

Like a model built ▶▶ on a tabletop, *Disneyland* Park in 1955 awaits the addition of attractions and the growth of the landscape— as well as the surrounding neighbors that the Park's success would bring.

A world of tomorrow being built in 1955.

Walt wanted a riverboat for his new park, and so he funded the construction of the *Mark Twain Riverboat* Attraction himself.

the baker write his name in icing on his birthday cake. Down one of the side streets is The Little Church Around the Corner. Nearby you will see the Mayor's House . . . a boarding house for guests and a Little Old Red School House. . . . Continuing along Main Street past the intriguing shops, you arrive at the Hub.

The Hub

The Hub is the crossroads of the world of Disneyland. Straight ahead lies Fantasy Land, to your left is Frontier Country, The World of Yesterday— and to your right is The World of Tomorrow. But between these central spokes of the wheel are other exciting avenues of adventure.

True-Life Adventureland

True-Life Adventureland is entered through a beautiful botanical garden of tropical flora and fauna. Here you can see magnificently plumed birds and fantastic fish from all over the world, and which may be purchased and shipped anywhere in the U.S. if you so desire. If you wish refreshments that are in keeping with your surroundings, there are fresh pineapple sticks, crisp coconut

meats, and exotic fruit punches made from fresh tropical fruits.

A river borders the edge of True-Life Adventureland, where you embark in a colorful Explorer's Boat with a native guide for a cruise down the River of Romance. As you glide through the Everglades, past birds and animals living in their natural habitat . . . alligators lurk along the banks, and otters and turtles play in the water about you. Monkeys chatter in the orchid-flowered trees.

The World of Tomorrow

A Moving Sidewalk carries you effortlessly into the World of Tomorrow where the fascinating exhibits of the miracles of science and industry are displayed. The theme for the World of Tomorrow is the factual and scientific exposition of Things to Come.

Participating in this are the Industries such as: Transportation, Rubber, Steel, Chemical, Electrical, Oil, Mining, Agriculture, and Foods.

Among the exhibits, that will change from time to time, are The Mechanical Brain . . . A Diving Bell . . . Monorail Train.

. . . The Little Parkway system where children drive scale-model motor cars over a modern freeway . . . Models of an atomic submarine, a Flying Saucer . . . The Magic House of Tomorrow, with mechanical features that obey the command of your voice like a Genie. You say "Please" and the door opens, a polite "Thank you" will close it.

When you enter the gigantic Rocket Space Ship to the Moon, and are safety-belted to your seat, the trip through "space" will be scientifically correct. The roaring ride through the universe will depict the exploding stars, constellations, planets, and comets exactly as charted, and be no less thrilling for being authentic.

Fantasy Land

Fantasy Land is a wonderful land of fairy tales come true within the walls and grounds of a great medieval castle whose towers loom seventy feet in the air. In the middle of the Castle grounds stands a magnificent carousel in the theme of King Arthur and his Knights. In this land of fantasy we find the settings from the fairy tales.

Ride through Snow White's adventures in the Seven Dwarfs mining car . . . through the diamond mines—the enchanted forest—past the cottage of the Seven Dwarfs reliving Snow White's adventures.

Walk through the wonderful experiences of Alice In Wonderland, as the White Rabbit takes you down the rabbit-hole, through the maze of doors, the Rabbit's House, past The Singing Flowers, Dodo Rock, the Mad Hatter's Tea Party, climaxing in the courtroom of the Queen of Hearts.

Fly through the air with Peter Pan, over London . . . past Big Ben clock . . . beyond the second star to the right for Never-Never Land.

Frontier Country

Where the Stagecoach meets the Train and the Riverboat for its trip down the river to New Orleans.

Along Frontier Street is a Harness Shop and a Blacksmith Shop, Livery Stable, Assayer's office, Sheriff's Office, and the jail. You can get real Western food at the Chuck Wagon, and cowboy clothes, six-shooters, or a silver-mounted saddle for your horse or pony at the General Store.

There is a shooting gallery, the Wells Fargo Express office, and an old-fashioned saloon with the longest little bar in the world serving root beer Western style.

At the end of Frontier Street is the boat-landing for the Riverboat Ride. The old stern-wheeler takes you downstream on a nostalgic cruise past the romantic river towns, Tom Sawyer's birthplace, and the old Southern plantations.

Disneyland will be the essence of America as we know it . . . the nostagia of the past, with exciting glimpses into the future. . . . And, mostly, as stated at the beginning— it will be a place for people to find happiness and knowledge. ■

Herb Ryman's fanciful concept drawing of Sleeping Beauty Castle became a more solid design, and then a construction project. *Sleeping Beauty* production designer Eyvind Earle tests color concepts in the WED model shop.

A Midwestern civic opera house rises from the sandy groveland of Anaheim, 1955.

"Well, it took many years. ... I started with many ideas, threw them away, started all over again. And eventually it evolved into what you see today at Disneyland."

—Walt Disney

The coveted Opening Day admission ticket to Walt Disney's latest ambitious enterprise.

Walt observes the ▶ final stages of his park's completion in July 1955.

Television was the keystone of the public acceptance of *Disneyland* Park. Through his weekly living room forum, Walt introduced audiences to the concepts of the Park, and elaborated on the themes of each of the "lands" to be explored.

1955–1965

Disneyland Realized

It was not very long ago, but a lifetime away. The America of 1955 was still dealing with the repercussions of the World War that had ended a decade earlier. Domestic harmony, strong family, a sense of cultural identity, and a genuine feeling of personal safety and national security were the desirable—but frequently elusive—dreams of most Americans.

The Disney Studio was enjoying a renewed creative vigor and financial security after a long period of uncertainty. Animated features such as *Cinderella* (1950), *Alice in Wonderland* (1951), *Peter Pan* (1953), and *Lady and the Tramp* (1955) had re-established Disney's preeminence in the field.

Although theatrical animated shorts starring Disney's stable of beloved standard characters had ceased regular production, there was a steady flow of special animation being created alongside the features, and the characters were reaching a whole new audience through the infant medium of television.

Unlike other studio heads, Walt saw huge potential in television and (as with all new media) was excited by it. The prospect of television's rewards far outweighed any fears that it might cannibalize his other ventures. Unlike many of his contemporaries, Walt seems to have immediately sensed the way in which a Disney TV presence could enhance and build upon his core culture, and aid in the expansion of his creative opportunities and avenues of communication.

The park he had envisioned for so long became the nucleus of his first TV venture, introduced his unusual and innovative project to a national audience, and immediately connected it with the beloved stories, movies, music, and memories of that audience's personal and collective culture. The excitement and anticipation for *Disneyland* Park as a destination was carefully built over the course of a year. No circus ever had a more ambitious or clever advance man than the one created by television for *Disneyland* Park.

And finally, when that long-dreamed-of Opening

◀◀ Even as *Disneyland* Park is completed, Walt works on plans for its expansion.

Just weeks before Opening Day, Sleeping Beauty Castle receives its final regal fittings.

The Red Wagon Inn once offered one of several unique dining opportunities in *Disneyland* Park. Today it is known as the Plaza Inn.

Day came, Walt rewarded his TV audience with a live, 90-minute broadcast spectacle, "Dateline: Disneyland," aired over the ABC Network and seen by almost every household that owned a television.

That first year was a shaky one for the new enterprise. An unprecedented heat wave with temperatures over one hundred degrees kept the summer business at a trickle. But the Park gained its footing, and soon an undeniable momentum. By 1957, 20 million visitors had come through the turnstiles.

That same year, Walt Disney Productions bought out the financial interests of ABC Television, Western Printing and Lithography, and even Walt Disney's personal share. *Disneyland* Park was now a wholly owned subsidiary.

It was also quickly becoming a Southern California gathering spot, with top events and performers such as the *Dixieland at Disneyland* show, the Disneyland Grad Nite Party, and beloved holiday events such as the Easter Parade, Christmas Parade, and the Candlelight Processional.

Television continued to be key to the Park's identity. Local Los Angeles station KTTV-TV aired a weekly series called "Meet Me at Disneyland." The original *Mickey Mouse Club* was re-edited and repackaged for syndication in 1962. The nation was always updated on news from *Disneyland* Park by way of the weekly Disney television hour, which featured programs such as "Disneyland After Dark," "Holiday Time at Disneyland," and "Disneyland Goes to the World's Fair."

In a short ten years, "Disneyland" had become cultural shorthand: a fantasy realm ("He's in his own little Disneyland"), an escape from the disagreeable, and most of all, an experience devoutly to be wished, a desirable destination for young and old, all around the world. ■

From the day it opened, *Disneyland* Park began to expand. The *Matterhorn Bobsleds* Attraction, inspired by the 1959 Disney feature *Third Man on the Mountain*, was a major addition to the Anaheim skyline.

BIT O' SWITZERLAND... THE MATTERHORN & SKYWAY

By 1959, *Disneyland*
Park had already
added dynamic new
attractions including
the *Matterhorn
Bobsleds* Attraction
and the first daily
operating monorail
system in the United
States. Just adjacent
to the mundane
traffic of Harbor
Boulevard was an
expanding world of
unparalleled enter-
tainment.

Detail is everywhere in *Disneyland* Park. Every element, no matter how seemingly minor, works as part of an enhancement to the overall perception and experience of the Park. When once asked about the abundance of seemingly superfluous detail, Walt Disney agreed that much of it goes unnoticed—but the *absence* of it would be apparent.

Sleeping Beauty Castle had become a Disney icon years before the release of its namesake animated feature. Details from the film were incorporated during construction and in the years since.

The seemingly incompatible icons of a miniature Swiss mountain bathing in the warm California sunset, in the company of festive balloons and a beloved cartoon duck, all seem to make sense at *Disneyland* Park.

◀◀ A microcosm of the *Disneyland* Park experience: friendly and familiar faces, colorful and unique surroundings, stirring music—and the ability to be a part of it all.

ride the **MINE TRAIN** thru NATURE'S WOND.

RIVERS OF AMERICA

OLYMPIC E.

BEAR COUNTRY

BEAVER VALLEY

PACK MULE TRAIL

RLAND

G DESERT

RAINBOW CAVERNS

of new attractions in
NEYLAND '60

"I don't want the public to see the world they live in while they're in the Park. I want them to feel they're in another world."

—Walt Disney

The 1960 addition of the elaborate *Mine Train Through Nature's Wonderland* had its origins in a hand-drawn sketch by Walt Disney himself.

CLOCKWISE FROM TOP LEFT: Things that aren't here anymore—the Frito Kid at Casa de Fritos, the Mickey Mouse Club Theater, House of the Future, live Mermaids in Submarine Lagoon, Viewliner train, and Main Street Bandstand.

"It was marvelous watching him with little kids down at the Park who would recognize him and come running up, and how gentle and caring he was with them."

—*Alice Davis, Imagineer*

The timeless quality of *Disneyland* Park. Two attractions that continue to thrill new visitors, more than five decades after their debut.

The Graphics Department at Walt Disney Imagineering has created dozens of award-winning attraction posters over the years.

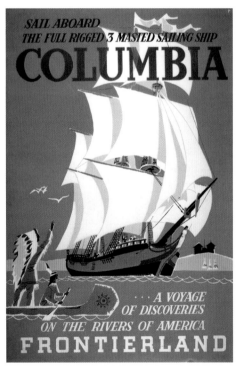

THE DISNEY SECRET

Disneyland Park used individual admission and attraction tickets from 1955 until 1981.

From "Disneyland Reports on its First Ten Million"
The New York Times
Sunday, February 2, 1958

By Gladwin Hill

What is the secret of Disneyland's success? Many factors have entered into it. But to pinpoint a single element, it would be imagination—not just imagination on the part of its impresarios, but their evocation of the imagination of the cash customers.

Walt Disney and his associates have managed to generate, in the traditionally raucous and ofttimes shoddy amusement park field, the same "suspension of disbelief" which has success down the corridors of time.

Everybody knows that relationships behind the footlights are simulated, that beneath a clown's ridiculous visage there is a human face, that Snow White is only a two-dimensional figure projected on a screen.

Similarly on Disneyland's popular African-River boat ride, a hard-bitten realist could point out that the boat is obviously on a track, that the jungle is a planted one, and that the animals and savages are mechanical. No F. B. I. man is needed to detect that another "river," which floats the big stern-wheeler Mark Twain, meanders no more than a couple of city blocks; or that throughout the rocket trip to the moon one's seat is firmly anchored to the ground. The point is that nobody wants to shatter illusions.

Theatrical artistry has been brought to bear so cleverly that the gates of Disneyland simply bar out the everyday world. Within the gates the park's entrance mall—the "Main Street" of 1900 America—leads to a circular array of realms of imagination. These are the tropical Adventureland, a pioneer-days Frontierland, a medieval Fantasyland, and a futuristic Tomorrowland. Once within them, the visitor indulges eagerly in that most ancient of games: "Let's pretend."

Grown-Ups, Too

Disneyland is not a new dictatorship of juvenile fancy, imposed on hapless grown-up escorts. In fact, its patronage runs a steady ratio of more than three adults to every child. Not infrequently, a compartment on one of the miniature streamlined trains can be seen occupied by a solitary oldster, lost in imagination. Visiting Russians have abruptly dropped their studied taciturnity to ride gleefully behind the bars of the Monkey Wagon on the toy circus train, heedless of any diplomatic repercussions. Parents scramble through the caves, tunnels, tree house, and stockade of Tom Sawyer's Island as avidly as their children.

While practically anyone who wants to go canoeing can do it fairly close to home any time, at Disneyland people line up to pay thirty-five cents for a few minutes paddling along the man-made vest-pocket "Mississippi." But this is in an Indian war canoe, with real Indians, bow and stern, controlling the exertions of a score of amateur paddlers at a time. Imagination again.

In the theatre the vital ingredient is not realism, but a blending of the real with the imaginary. The entertainer invites the audience to meet him half way. This is what has been successfully achieved at Disneyland. ■

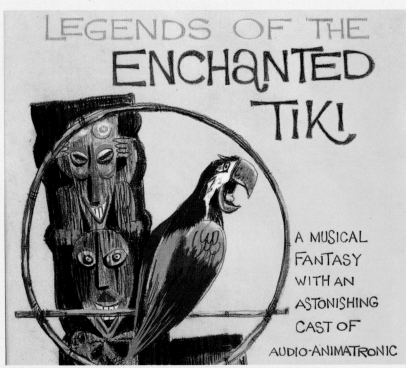

◄◄ When soldiers returned home from World War II, they brought with them the lore and romance of the South Seas. Americans fell in love with the romanticized version of this exotic culture, and Polynesian design began to infuse every aspect of the American aesthetic—and *Disneyland* Park was no different.

"I first saw the site for Disneyland back in 1953. In those days it was all flat land—no rivers, no mountains, no castles or rocket ships—just orange groves, and a few acres of walnut trees."

—*Walt Disney*

As stated in the original *Disneyland* Park Proposal in 1954, "Here is Adventure. Here is Romance. Here is Mystery... we pictured ourselves far from civilization, in the remote jungles of Asia and Africa." Cinematic exotica and pop culture mystery await, just beyond this portal.

"The architects and engineers agreed, 'It can't be done.'
Walt just smiled, and it was done. That was that."

—*Harriet Burns, Imagineer*

◀◀ The Flight Circle
(1955–1965) in
Tomorrowland Area
was the home of
hobby airplane
demonstrations, first
as the Wen-Mac
Flight Circle, then as
the Thimble Drome
Flight Circle operated
by the L.M. Cox
Company.

Today it's *Star Tours*
Attraction, but from
1955 to 1966, the
Monsanto Hall of
Chemistry exhibit
featured The Chemi-
tron, demonstrating
the origin of 500
different Monsanto
chemicals and
plastics.

The 1959 *Tomorrow-land* Area expansion saw the addition of attractions that delight visitors today as they have millions in the past: the *Matterhorn Bobsleds* Attraction, the *Disneyland Monorail*, and the *Submarine Voyage* Attraction.

THE DISNEYLAND STORY

From *Walt Disney's America*, 1978

By Christopher Finch

It is worth taking a detailed look at the genesis and planning of Disneyland because its completion was one of the milestones of Walt Disney's career, and the story tells us much about the way the man thought and worked. In particular, we can see how his major ideas tended to grow out of his own life experience and his response to his native environment.

Amusement parks were not a novelty in Southern California. For many years, the piers at Venice, Ocean Park, and Santa Monica were the sites of large amusement areas of the Coney Island type, complete with sideshows, fun houses, giant roller coasters, and all the traditional midway attractions. In the silent era, these often provided a background for Hollywood movies. By the late forties, however, most of these operations had fallen on hard times or had been closed down entirely. The public was demanding something more sophisticated, and most entrepreneurs interpreted this as meaning that all amusement parks were doomed to eventual extinction. Disney thought otherwise. His interpretation of the phenomenon was that people wanted a different kind of amusement park, but he found few professionals who would agree with him. When he

was researching the feasibility of Disneyland, he sent aides all over the country, seeking the advice of acknowledged experts in the field. The advice these experts handed out was unanimous: "Forget about building an amusement park. It's certain to be a disaster." Disney recalled that other experts had predicted that *Snow White* would be a failure and pressed ahead with his scheme.

Disney had been thinking about his park for a very long time. When his daughters were youngsters, he often took them to a little amusement area on La Cienega Boulevard where they had a good time but he found himself becoming bored. "I'd sit," he once explained, "while they rode the merry-go-round and did all those things—sit on a bench, you know, eating peanuts. I felt there should be something built where the parents and the children could have fun together. So that's how Disneyland started . . . it was a period of maybe fifteen years developing."

During this period of gestation, he modified his plans many times. At first he seems to have thought of a modest playground at the studio itself, one that would feature rides built around Disney characters. Nothing came of this, though it was a project he was fond of talking about. Impetus for a rather grander kind of park came in part from a hobby that Disney took up right after the war.

Walt had always been fascinated by railroads. Trains were one of his boyhood obsessions and, when his doctor suggested that he was working too hard and needed a hobby, he turned back to that world. (Until shortly before the war, he had played polo for relaxation, but his backers eventually insisted that he give up the sport, fearing that he might be seriously injured.) Two of Disney's top animators, Ward Kimball and Ollie Johnston, were already serious railroad buffs, and Walt picked up many tips from them, then began to construct his own backyard railroad, building much of the rolling stock with his own hands.

In the early years of the studio, Disney had had plenty of opportunities to use his hands—some department always needed help to meet a deadline—but gradually these evaporated as he found himself more and more involved with the conceptual side of filmmaking. Building his miniature railroad restored to him a valued activity; but inevitably, given his imagination, it also evoked a whole new range of possibilities. He must have remembered the roar of the big Santa Fe locomotives as they rushed through Marceline, the excitement of the small-town depot. Before long, he was talking about running a railroad around the Burbank Studio, and soon this impulse became attached to his notion of a new kind of amusement park. Transportation and nostalgia, he saw, could be a big factor in making his park different.

Between the Disney lot and the Los Angeles River was a tract of undeveloped land which today

It was his love of trains that led Walt Disney to become a railroad hobbyist, and his 1948 visit to the Chicago railroad fair took him to Henry Ford's Greenfield Village.

"Our whole forty-some odd years here has been in the world of making things move, inanimate things move. From a drawing to all kinds of any little props and things. Now we're, uh, making these, uh, human figures, dimensional human figures move, make animals move, make anything move, through the use of electronics."

—*Walt Disney*

carries a stretch of the Ventura Freeway, and Walt thought about acquiring this for his scheme, but he decided it was not large enough. Once committed to an idea, he was incapable of not developing it to its logical conclusion, and the concept of Disneyland began to expand in his mind and on paper until it became evident that a site of two or three hundred acres would be required.

At this point, Disney commissioned the Stanford Research Institute to scout locations for him. The institute's recommendation was that he purchase a large tract of orange groves in Anaheim, south of Los Angeles, close to the proposed route of the Santa Ana Freeway which was then under construction. At that time, Anaheim was relatively isolated, but the freeway would bring it within a short drive of the major Los Angeles residential neighborhoods, while Orange County, where Anaheim is situated, was rapidly becoming urbanized too.

The site was perfect for Disney's purposes, and his plans for the park began to take definitive shape. (Eventually, a new corporation, WED—for Walter Elias Disney—was set up to supervise the planning.) There remained the matter of financing the park and this, given the experts' doubts about its feasibility, was not an easy matter.

Disney put much of his own money into the early planning of Disneyland, even selling his weekend

home in Palm Springs to raise cash, but major backers were needed, and eventually two companies came forward with the funding. One was Western Printing and Lithography, a publishing company that had had a long association with the Disney organization. The other was the American Broadcasting Company.

In the early fifties, ABC was running a distant third to NBC and CBS in the rapidly developing television market. All three networks had approached Disney with a view to having him originate a series for them. He had agreed to produce a couple of specials but had fought the series idea, perhaps because he had had bad luck with a radio series several years earlier. ABC, however, had much to gain by persuading Disney to join its lineup and finally an agreement was reached. Disney would produce the *Disneyland* series for ABC and, in return, ABC would put up a substantial amount of capital to help finance the park. Since the series would help promote the park, this seemed satisfactory all around. Disney had already persuaded thirty companies to lease concessions in the proposed park, which brought in more capital, and Walt Disney Productions was able to raise a sum equal to the ABC investment. Eventually, acting on a prior agreement, the Disney organization bought out both ABC and Western.

Disneyland opened in July of 1955, and it soon

Although a far-flung
vacation destination
for millions, *Disney-
land* Park has always
relied on local visitors
for more than half
its population. Clever
locally targeted
advertisements have
been a staple for
decades.

"Disneyland is a thing that I can keep molding 'play with it,' I don't mean that. Everything

became clear that it would be a great success. From this point on, the Disney organization would have few financial worries and Walt Disney himself, finally, would become a wealthy man, though he did not change his modest lifestyle.

Disneyland was far more than just a financial triumph, however; it was a totally new kind of entertainment complex and it was to become a symbol of the age—the ultimate American pleasure ground, a kind of permanent Fourth of July celebration. A few quotes will serve to show exactly what Walt Disney was aiming for when he built the first of his Magic Kingdoms:

> "Disneyland is like Alice stepping through the looking glass. To step through the portals of Disneyland will be like entering another world."

> "Disneyland would be a world of Americans, past and present, seen through the eyes of my imagination—a place of warmth and nostalgia, of illusion and color and delight."

> "Disneyland will be the essence of America as we know it, the nostalgia of the past with exciting glimpses of the future. It will give meaning to the pleasure of children—and pleasure to the experience of adults . . . It will be a place for the people to find happiness and knowledge."

The layout of the park was an important factor contributing to its success, as Disney clearly recognized:

> "The more I go to other amusement parks . . . the more I am convinced of the wisdom of the original concept of Disneyland. I mean, have a single entrance through which all the traffic would flow, then a hub off which the various areas were situated. This gives people a sense of orientation—they know where they are at all times. And it saves a lot of walking."

These practical considerations were important, but so was the symbolism since, as already noted, the single entrance opened onto Town Square and Main Street, and Main Street became the way into Adventureland, Fantasyland, Frontierland, and Tomorrowland. The layout of Disneyland is like a diagram of Walt Disney's imagination.

No matter how well the park was conceived, however, it would not have worked if the plan had not been executed with a sharp sense of quality and detail. People visiting Disneyland for the first time are often surprised by the craftsmanship which is evident on all sides. This is a world of illusion, but the props are startlingly real, and we must remember that the movie industry has had long experience in conjuring up other times and other places. The Western towns and European squares that can be found on Hollywood back lots may consist of nothing but false fronts attached to crude frameworks, but they are remarkably convincing. Disneyland is, in fact, like a gigantic back lot open to the public, with the important differ-

> and shaping. It's a three-dimensional thing to play with. But when I say, I do I keep a practical eye towards its appeal to the public." —*Walt Disney*

ence that its false façades conceal rides and entertainments rather than storage space for generators and lighting equipment.

We must realize, too, that the people who planned Disneyland—from Walt Disney down—were mostly men who had spent their life in the movie industry. Many were graduates of the animation department. They brought to the park the same imagination that they had brought to screen entertainment. Characters and situations developed in Disney movies also provided the basis for many of the park's rides.

Everything has been carefully considered. The scale of Main Street has been subtly altered—the upper stories are not quite as tall as they would be in a real town—so that a feeling of intimacy is produced (especially in contrast to the glass-and-steel canyons of modern cities). Main Street makes visitors feel a little larger than life. The architecture is not a pastiche of turn-of-the-century styles—it is an immaculate reproduction. No corners have been cut. Every detail, down to the last piece of gingerbread fretwork, is made exactly as it would have been made in 1900. The charming art of the sign painter is everywhere in evidence, and the vintage cars and horse-drawn trolleys are exactly what you might have seen in any American town in the early years of the century. (Disney made a deliberate decision to capture the brief period in which the automobile had arrived but had not yet displaced the horse-drawn vehicle.)

Walt Disney had a hard childhood and knew as well as anyone else that "the good old days" were not all good, but he also understood that they take on a new significance as they slip into the past. Memory tends to strip the past of its quotidian hardships while abstracting the positive values that transcend the shifts of circumstance. Disney made every effort to sharpen our picture of the past by focusing on those details which seem significant in retrospect. Disneyland's Main Street and the adjacent Town Square area (which Walt could survey from his private apartment above the fire station) are designed to evoke old values, a sense of neighborhood, and the compactness of society in a simpler age.

Walt Disney was a conservative man in that he believed that such old values retain their usefulness, if only as a reminder of what was once viable. I think it is fair to say that, for him, Main Street was a metaphor for a way of life governed by what can only be called common sense, and his belief in the validity of common sense permeated everything he did. Of course, the paradox of Disney is that his common-sense approach was always allied with a highly developed instinct for the creation of fantasy. It is the fantasy that lends an aura of enchantment to the Magic Kingdom—what other Main Street leads to a castle from the once-upon-a-time world of the Brothers Grimm?—but the fact that it is rooted in easily understood values makes the fabulous all the more accessible to the millions of visitors who enjoy it annually. ■

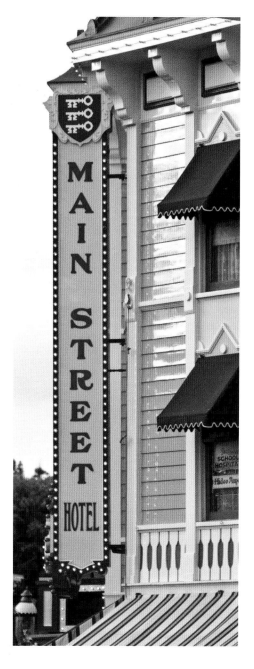

Signs and placards, both vintage and cutting edge, are a hallmark of *Disneyland* Park detail, and a special treat for graphic design and commercial art aficionados.

An elegant riverboat was part of Walt's earliest plans for a park. When it was built in 1955, the ⅝-scale sternwheeler *Mark Twain* was the first functional riverboat to be built in the United States in more than fifty years.

DISNEYLAND–SCAPING WITH BILL EVANS

From *Disneyland World of Flowers*, 1965

By Morgan "Bill" Evans

"I wanted something alive, something that could grow . . . even the trees will keep growing. The thing will get more beautiful each year!"
—*Walt Disney*

It took magic of a sort to transform 165 acres of flat, windswept land in Anaheim, California, into Disneyland, a Magic Kingdom of mountains, lakes, forests, lawns, and gardens known the world over.

Even when Disneyland was still just a series of sketches and plans, Walt Disney was keenly aware of the importance of imaginative landscaping in the Park. Today, Disneyland's horticultural display charms visitors with its unusual plants from around the world.

During the hectic months in 1955 when Disneyland was being completed, and in the years following,

plants from many lands were collected and moved into the Park. With few exceptions, they have survived the transplanting and have thrived in their new home. Some trees have put on so much growth, in fact, that it would be impossible to move them again. Guests strolling through the Park today may find it hard to believe that only a few years ago there was nothing to see there but row upon row of orange trees.

After the decision was made to purchase the land in Anaheim for the Park, our first chore was to remove the citrus trees and clear the stage for huge earth-moving equipment that would reshape the resulting wasteland.

Walt Disney's Magic Kingdom was conceived to provide an escape from the cares of today into the

nostalgia of the past, the excitement of the future, and the wonderful realm of fantasy. An important step toward this objective was the visual exclusion of the twentieth century by the construction of a twenty-foot "berm," a mound of earth completely surrounding the Park. The separation was further effected by dense plantings of trees and shrubs atop the berm, which today form the horizon in many vistas from inside Disneyland.

Bulldozers, turnapulls, and other giant equipment excavated and hauled approximately one million tons of earth to build the berm and sculpture the mountains, valleys, rivers, streams, and waterfalls envisaged by Walt Disney.

The landscape department followed in the wake of the bulldozers, transforming the arid scene into assorted jungles, forests, gardens, and lawns. First came the big trees, their roots packaged in heavy boxes. Some weighed as much as twenty-two tons. Then came the smaller trees, shrubs, vines, and the irrigation systems to supply the rainfall for these plants from faraway lands. At the last minute came the flowers (already in full bloom from the greenhouses) and the grass, which was unrolled carpetlike as fully established lawns.

Anaheim enjoys a congenial climate, but the summers are warm enough to make some shade very welcome. Shade trees of appropriate size and variety are not in ample supply in Southern California; Disneyland's needs soon exhausted the available stock from commercial nurseries. It was necessary to turn to old gardens and estates, sometimes hundreds of miles distant, for additional specimens. California's projected freeways, routed unavoidably

Beloved Disney
characters find
permanent homes
amid the lush
greenery.

through residential districts, afforded an unusual opportunity to salvage full-grown trees. Former owners can take some comfort from the knowledge that many fine specimens were literally snatched from the jaws of the bulldozers, then packaged and transported to Disneyland for a new lease on life. Here, spreading their branches against the sky, they lend shelter to bird and man, and contribute graceful beauty for millions to enjoy.

From the very beginning, Walt Disney insisted upon plenty of trees to provide shade for the Park's guests, and we miss no opportunity to augment the number. The objective is not without problems, however: where to put the additional trees? Shade is a must, but we also need sunshine for lawns and flower beds. Furthermore, we cannot afford to obstruct the pathways or the view of the authentic detailing on buildings which contributes so much interest and charm to Disneyland. For these reasons we are approaching a saturation

point with large trees in most of the public areas. Disneyland's landscaping covers a broad spectrum, from a simulated Congo rain forest in Adventureland to the contemporary display gardens surrounding Monsanto's House of Tomorrow. Walt Disney requested year-round color, and the landscape department has managed to spread before our guests a perennial welcome mat of flowers. Whether the season be spring, summer, autumn, or winter, one may visit Disneyland at three-month intervals and find the same flower beds in bloom but displaying different varieties each time. From the time the visitor enters the main parking area, which is banked with colorful oleanders, until his departure from the Magic Kingdom, he will seldom be out of camera range of flowers.

Over half a million annuals are set out each year, carefully scheduled and grown to order by local nurserymen. Over 750 different species and varieties of plants are permanent residents of the Park. Most are

of interest to the home gardener; some only to the horticulturist or student of botany. A few are unique, perhaps not in cultivation elsewhere in this country.

Pleasant weather is the general rule in Disneyland, and though rain is infrequent we do have some hot days and a few cold nights. Fortunately, people have devised effective means of adapting themselves to seasonal climatic changes. Our plant charges, on the other hand, are like children who cannot fend for themselves and must be protected from getting wet, cold, and even dry, feet. They require shelter from sun and windburn as well as frostbite. So in addition to irrigation systems, the landscape department has provided hot wind machines to churn the chilling air of winter nights, modifying the discouraging effects of cold temperatures on tender specimens. . . .

No commentary on Disneyland landscaping would be complete without reference to maintenance and cultural practices.

Like every home gardener, but on a much larger scale, we keep up an unending battle against the vagaries of weather, a host of insect pests, and an assortment of fungus diseases. The welfare of our plants in the Park demands constant vigilance on the part of competent gardeners who, if not seen, are nonetheless ever-present. ■

In 1952, third-generation horticulturist Bill Evans landscaped the grounds of Walt Disney's home, including the gardens that surrounded his backyard railroad. In 1954, Walt asked Bill and his brother, Jack, to supervise landscaping at Disneyland Park. Bill was named director of landscape architecture, working on Disneyland Park additions and the master plan for Walt Disney World Resort, and consulting on the landscape design of Tokyo Disneyland Park. He has also consulted on Disneyland Resort Paris as well as on the schematic designs of Epcot®, Disney's Hollywood Studios, and Disney's Animal Kingdom Theme Park, and on dozens of other elements of the Florida resort.

◀◀ *Much like the wilds of the Jungle River of Adventureland Area, the Critter Country Area landscape is designed for an appearance of a more "woodsy" nature in its more raw state.*

The Belgian and Percheron geldings that draw the *Main Street, U.S.A.* Streetcars work four hours a day, four days a week.

The longest-running *Frontierland* Area show, Golden Horseshoe Revue, made its home here from July 17, 1955 to October 12, 1986.

A unique glimpse from a storybook past toward an American past that becomes more and more the stuff of fantasy.

1965–1975

Tencennial

In all the world, there is but one Disneyland. Here, in a decade's time, 50 million guests from the Earth's four corners have come to participate in adventures unique in all the world. For here, tomorrow is today, and yesterday is forever.

In all the world, there is but one Disneyland. Yet Disneyland is many different worlds, by day and by night, for every age and every mood. It is 1890 again on Main Street, U.S.A. and 1980 in Tomorrowland. It is the pioneer's hardy realm, Frontierland, and a jungle safari to far-off worlds in Adventureland. And it is a castle full of dreams—the classic tales of childhood "come to life" in Fantasyland.

To Walt Disney's Magic Kingdom in these ten years has come a royal procession of kings and queens, a diplomatic corps of presidents and prime ministers. And with them, from more than one hundred nations and America's fifty states, you have come—the young at heart of all ages to join the daytime fun and nighttime magic of Walt Disney's Magic Kingdom.

If you, too, are among the young at heart, come with us on a journey 'round this world … the Many Worlds of Disneyland.
—*Disneyland* Park Tencennial
Promotional Supplement

As the second decade of *Disneyland* Park began, the abundance and momentum of social and political change in the United States and throughout the world continued. Even as Lyndon B. Johnson was inaugurated as U.S. President on a legislative program of national reform known as "The Great Society," there were race riots in the Los Angeles area of Watts, and Black Power movement leader Malcolm X was assassinated.

U.S. air raids in Vietnam began, and anti-war protests in the U.S. and Europe began in kind. The gulf between generations widened. Complacency and conservatism clashed with anxiety and activism.

Disneyland Park, however, maintained a soverign culture where all were at peace, all could find something to agree about. The Magic Kingdom began

◄◄ Walt Disney and Tencennial Ambassador Julie Reihm peruse the Plaza Inn model under the watchful eye of Disney Legend Harriet Burns.

Yes, that's right. The giant Tencennial birthday cake would slice itself and dance as part of the celebration.

The plans for a ►► "Haunted House" had been in the works since 1953, and the *Haunted Mansion* Attraction exterior was built in 1963, but foolish mortals would not tour these happy haunting grounds until 1969.

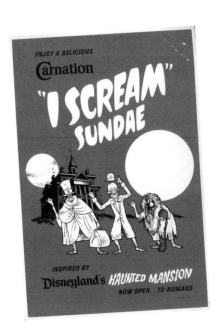

the tumultuous decade with a birthday party, dubbed the "Tencennial." And there was much to celebrate.

"Today Disneyland has forty-eight major attractions," a 1965 article written by Walt Disney read, "and represents an investment of more than $52 million. That's a long way from the little park we first started laying out, or even the $17 million Magic Kingdom we opened in July of 1955.

"Today the Disneyland 'navy' has more than eighty vessels—about as many as the British fleet that chased the great Spanish Armada. And our submarine fleet is the eighth largest in the world.

"In just a decade, Disneyland has more than doubled in number of attractions . . . and I guess you could say we're just starting. Right now, the creative imagination of our staff is busy dreaming up adventures that will cost three times as much to build as all of Disneyland did 10 years ago.

"Many of these attractions will 'come to life' through Audio-Animatronics, our space-age electronic method of making inanimate things move on cue, hour after hour and show after show. We first introduced it in the Enchanted Tiki Room where birds tell jokes, flowers croon, and Tikis chant in a seventeen-minute theatre show.

"This summer, Audio-Animatronics will enable us to present the inspiring words of our sixteenth President, Abraham Lincoln, in a new and dramatic way that has lasting impact and meaning for young and old alike. I hope you will plan to spend a few 'Great Moments with Mr. Lincoln' on your next visit to the Magic Kingdom.

"The Lincoln show is our newest addition, but the way I see it, Disneyland will never be finished. It's something we can keep developing and adding to. A motion picture is different. Once it's wrapped up and sent out for processing, we're through with it. If there are things that could be improved, we can't do anything about them anymore.

"I've always wanted to work on something alive, something that keeps growing. We've got that in Disneyland."

Although *Disneyland* Park endured, Walt himself was gone by the end of the second year of the park's second decade. He had left plans and ideas enough to last for years, and a cultural and creative philosophy second to no other American business or cultural institution. Now it would be up to his creative heirs to succeed or fail, with only the tools of Walt's ideas and the inspirational gift of his memory. ■

The Main Street
Electrical Parade
ran during summer
1972–1974,
1977–1982,
and 1985–1996.
The new Disney's
Electrical Parade
began at *Disney's
California Adventure*
Park in 2001.

What began as a ▶▶
"Wax Museum of
Piracy" in 1957
became a popular
Disneyland Park
attraction in 1967
and a blockbuster
film series in 2003.
A Jack Sparrow
Audio-Animatronics
Figure was added
in 2006.

"In big cities, everything is out of place. There are contradictions, where there's a lack of harmony with things. I think Walt was very aware of the small details that would intrude and offer contradiction."

—*John Hench, Imagineer*

it's a small world debuted at the 1964–1965 New York World's Fair at the UNICEF pavilion, celebrating the world's children. The happiest cruise that ever sailed is a favorite destination in all five *Magic Kingdom* Parks worldwide.

WALT DISNEY SPOKEN HERE

By Marty Sklar
Walt Disney Imagineering Ambassador

There may be no single location in the United States today more closely identified with a single individual than *Disney-*land Park. Even though its Florida cousin, *Walt Disney World* Resort, bears Walt Disney's entire name as its official "brand," the original Park in Anaheim, California, set the pattern for the ten future Disney parks around the world. And it is the only Disney park that Walt ever walked in.

Without Walt Disney's singular vision, his passion and dedication, his refusal to accept "no" for an answer to a new challenge, *Disneyland* Park would never have advanced beyond the sixty-eight master plans drawn by art director Marvin Davis before Walt OK'd the actual plan for a July 17, 1955 opening. The biggest amusement park operators in the country had told Walt's emissaries that a park with one entrance ("we have four"), a permanent staff ("too expensive"), and seasonally changed flower beds ("they'll get trampled") was doomed to failure. "Tell Walt to save his money," they admonished.

In its first decade, however, *Disneyland* Park became what one reporter called "almost an instrumentality of American foreign policy" as kings and queens, presidents and prime ministers, joined millions of Guests to soar with *Dumbo The Flying Elephant* Attraction, explore tropical jungles, and race to the moon and back. Author Ray Bradbury accompanied the great actor Charles Laughton to *Disneyland* Park and wrote: "Disney makes many mistakes; what artist doesn't? But when he flies, he really flies!" One of America's premier developers, James Rouse, called *Disneyland* Park "the greatest piece of urban design in America" in his keynote speech at the 1963 Urban Design Conference at Harvard University.

But for all his public accolades, Walt Disney's most significant contribution to the realms of fantasy and adventure and predictions for tomorrow in his parks may well have been his inspiration to the team of talents he called "Imagineers." Following Walt's death in 1966, the Imagineers he put in place nurtured and pushed to go beyond yesterday. Designers, engineers, artists, mechanical wizards, and so many more created the *Walt Disney World* Resort (including the *Magic Kingdom* Park and *Epcot*®) . . . launched the first-ever international Disney park in Tokyo, Japan . . . and set in motion the creation of seven

more Disney parks and resorts in Paris, Hong Kong, Florida, and California.

These remarkable creative talents were originally handpicked by Walt, and "cast" for their new assignments at Imagineering. Some, like John Hench, Marc Davis, Claude Coats, Herb Ryman, Sam McKim, Blaine Gibson, and Harper Goff, were mainstays on Disney films and animation, contributing to projects including *Snow White and the Seven Dwarfs*, *Dumbo*, *Peter Pan*, and *20,000 Leagues Under the Sea*. Others, like Richard Irvine, Marvin Davis, and Bill Martin, were veteran art directors who had proven their design skills in the Hollywood studio system. Almost universally, they had two uncommon genes in their artistic make-up: they were willing to try anything, and they did not know how to say "no." As Bob Gurr, designer of early *Disneyland* Park vehicles, fresh out of Art Center College of Design, learned in his new "Disney classes" from day one: "You didn't say 'no' to Walt Disney, because he would find someone willing to take a chance."

My mentors, especially John Hench and Herb Ryman, were the true spirits of Imagineering for many years beyond

Walt's own lifetime. Herb's last illustrations for Disney parks came when he was in his seventies, for *Indiana Jones*™ *Adventure* Attraction, and the *Main Street, U.S.A.* Area for *Disneyland* Resort Paris—thirty-some years after drawing the very first overall illustration of *Disneyland* Park, with Walt literally looking over his shoulders, in 1953. John, who designed *Space Mountain* Attraction and Spaceship Earth at *Epcot*®, was the color guru of every Disney park, even helping to establish the Castle color scheme for *Hong Kong Disneyland* Resort. He was still working every day when he passed away at age ninety-four, in his sixty-third year at Disney.

Today, several generations of new Disney artists, designers, and creators owe their training, as I do, to the John Henches and Herb Rymans of Imagineering . . . thereby reaching across half a century back to the foundation—the original philosophy, storytelling magic, attitude toward the public ("you don't build it for yourself"), and inspiration of one man: Walt Disney. He did not need to walk in more than one park, the first *Disneyland* Park in California. His footprints are

everywhere, in all eleven Disney parks and beyond, around the world.

I think of it as the world's first international language. "Walt Disney spoken here" speaks volumes about optimism, passion, originality, risk-taking, learning, beauty, creativity and, without question, reassurance that you can actually speak to a stranger in a public place, admire a flower bed without trampling it, and more than anything, have fun with your family and friends. Enjoy your next visit, whether it's number one or, like me, numbers in the thousands! There are few experiences in life that create more anticipation of a great fun day than to say to your family, "We're going to Disneyland!" ■

Marty Sklar began his career with Disney in 1955, two weeks before the Opening Day of Disneyland *Park, and retired on July 17, 2009, the Park's 54th anniversary. He was named a Disney Legend in 2001.*

Greetings from
the future! The
Tomorrowland
Area spaceman
and his out-of-this-
world companion,
circa 1957.

Looking to the future. Walt Disney, perpetually gazing toward his next project, shares his vision with Mickey Mouse in the "Partners" sculpture, created by Disney Legend Blaine Gibson.

1975–1985

Traditional but Trendy

As the third decade began, the world kept turning, but *Disneyland* Park remained a constant of reassurance and safety in what seemed to be an increasingly polarized, violent, and dangerous time.

The People's Republic of China changed with the beginning of market liberalization, the economy of Japan witnessed a large boom (study of the economic aspects of a theme park in Japan began at Disney in 1975), and the United States withdrew its military forces from Vietnam as Saigon fell to communism. Violence in the Middle East had increased as Egypt and Syria declared war on Israel, and the situation in the Middle East was deeply changed by a peace agreement between Egypt and Israel. Political tensions in Iran exploded with the Iranian Revolution.

In the United States, the African American Civil Rights movement, although far from complete, had achieved many of its goals, and the Feminist movement took a prominent role in society.

True to the dreams of optimistic futurists like Walt Disney, technology continued to progress with the continuing development of solid-state physics and the integrated circuit.

Another of Walt's dreams, the exploration of space, continued. The ambitious Skylab fell to Earth in a blaze of glory, but the space shuttle program remained strong, and a variety of unmanned lunar and planetary probes were launched.

In popular culture overall, the innocence and simplicity of entertainment was undergoing an evolution. Stalwart stars and programming styles were supplanted by fare of more currency and social commentary, presenting an American culture less based on ideals and more focused on the changing societal roles and the evolving "traditional" views.

Venerable entertainment archetypes in both film and television experienced decline—picture palaces were closed and frequently razed, multiplexes and shopping mall cinemas took their functional place, but never their sentimental one.

◀◀ The iconic image of Mickey, Donald, and Goofy, recreating Archibald Willard's monumental 1876 painting *The Spirit of '76*, was first featured in the July 1939 issue of *Mickey Mouse Magazine*. It became the symbol of Disney's Bicentennial Celebration.

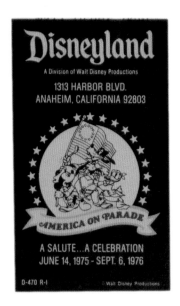

The American Bicentennial celebration was a popular cultural phenomenon, at once patriotic and nostalgic.

On screens large and small, Westerns, musicals, and variety shows were supplanted by police and detective dramas, situation comedies, science fiction, and what were politely termed "jiggle shows."

Soap operas and game shows, once the sole asset of daytime television, became a popular evening programming option, and the television "mini-series" enjoyed its heyday as the infant cable television industry began to fracture the "big three" network hierarchy.

For a creative organization based on history, tradition, and a perception of "values," this era of chaotic culture might certainly have been a difficult one. The management at Disney, however, began to realize that Disney was a unique culture all its own, one that transcended national boundaries and generations; and that by remaining true to that culture, Disney could remain strong in the face of any external, social, and political chaos.

Carefully, Disney management began to expand and enhance the idea of what "Disney" was, through the establishment of the Touchstone Pictures label for fare not specifically oriented to families with children; Disney Channel, a premium cable channel featuring classic and current Disney programming; and a prestige Home Video label. International expansion began with *Tokyo Disneyland* Resort, and *Walt Disney World* Resort in Florida celebrated ten years and opened a second theme park, EPCOT.

At *Disneyland* Park, a similar, careful, and consistent expansion beyond the core Disney properties was happening. The public taste for "thrill" rides saw more roller coasters come to *Disneyland* Park, but following in the tracks of Walt's own *Matterhorn Bobsleds* Attraction, *Space Mountain* Attraction and *Big Thunder Mountain Railroad* Attraction added extraordinary settings, effects, sound, and storylines rather than simple thrills.

At the same time, plans for a complete overhaul of the *Fantasyland* Area called not for a modernization, but a return to the palace courtyard, Bavarian Village, and English Towne of its fairy tale origins. Even in changing times, sometimes the best way to look to the future is to celebrate and honor the most beloved of the past.

Another decade, and another generation of Guests, meant an extension of the enduring tradition of *Disneyland* Park itself. Birthdays, first dates, Grad Nites, Christmas Parades, and concerts—all of them became an integral part of the lives of further generations who had never known a world without *Disneyland* Park. ■

Whatever their actual national origins, Disney Characters are distinctly American, especially when presented in a riot of red, white, and blue!

The cool blue dome and soaring spires of *Space Mountain* Attraction, still an optimistic architectural statement after more than thirty years, exemplify the timeless elegance of exceptional design.

FEELING GROOVY?
DISNEYLAND WEATHERS THE FAR-OUT 1970s

By Tim O'Day

In the 1970s, many wondered if *Disneyland* Park could successfully carry on without Walt's creative guidance or if it would succumb to the temptation to change with the times to be more "hip" and "groovy"?

Doubts vanished quickly as the Disney Imagineers and *Disneyland* Park Cast Members faced the dawning 1970s with even greater resolve. They steadfastly remained committed to Walt's values of innovation, imagination, and quality, thus guaranteeing that *Disneyland* Park would continue to evolve yet stay the cherished international landmark it had become.

Through careful evolution, *Disneyland* Park transcended fads and trends, continuing to be a place of reassuring escape from the chaotic world outside. It had become "cool" for just being itself.

The proven blueprint of *Disneyland* Park was successfully transported east, forming the basis for the *Magic Kingdom* Park at *Walt Disney World* Resort in Florida. During its development, it fell to countless *Disneyland* Cast Members to successfully train, open, and initially oversee the operation of this entirely new "Disney World."

Walt Disney World Resort became a reality thanks in large measure to those original "Disneylanders" who assisted Walt in making "The Happiest Place on Earth" a globally recognized showplace. On October 1, 1971, the all-new and significantly larger "Vacation Kingdom of the World" in Orlando was set on a course to create its own remarkable and distinct history.

New fun came to *Disneyland* Park as well. *America Sings*, a patriotic musical review, and the high-speed intergalactic adventure *Space Mountain* Attraction both opened in *Tomorrowland* Area, while "The Wildest Ride in the Wilderness"— *Big Thunder Mountain Railroad* Attraction (the first of its kind) debuted in *Frontierland* Area. The Main Street Electrical Parade began its twenty-four-year run as a beloved *Disneyland* Park spectacular, soon followed by the opening of *The Walt Disney Story* on *Main Street, U.S.A.* Area (later joined by the return of *Great Moments With Mr. Lincoln*).

Not content with just new shows and adventures, *Disneyland* Park unveiled an entirely new "land" called Bear Country (now known as *Critter Country* Area). Here Guests could enjoy the country-western musical antics of the

Country Bear Jamboree (the first attraction imported from *Walt Disney World* Resort).

A highlight of the decade was perhaps the largest single entertainment production ever produced for Disney parks. Conceived as a salute and a celebration honoring the American Bicentennial, *America on Parade* began daily performances in June 1975, at both *Disneyland* Park and the *Magic Kingdom* Park at *Walt Disney World* Resort, and continued until September 1976. In all, the elaborate red, white, and blue extravaganza completed more than 1,200 performances before a total live audience of twenty-five million, the largest audience ever to view a live performance.

By the end of the '70s, *Disneyland* Park was nearing its twenty-fifth anniversary. It had weathered both the loss of Walt Disney and vast cultural changes, welcomed well over 150 million guests, and cemented its reputation the world over as a "must-see" destination. ■

Tim O'Day is a creative and marketing executive with more than three decades of Disney experience, and he is a well-known authority on Disneyland Resort and its history.

THE GREATEST BUNCH OF CHARACTERS YOU'LL EVER MEET

From Disney News, Fall 1976

Eager hands reach out with love to touch them. Toddlers tug at their jackets, trousers, coattails. Shutterbugs call for them to look this way or that. Children call their names . . .

"There's Pluto . . . there's Brer Bear . . . there's the Seven Dwarfs . . . there's Mickey . . . " they shout happily as some of Walt Disney's best-loved cartoon creations step lively along Main Street, U.S.A., New Orleans Square, and throughout Disneyland.

There are nearly forty such Disney Characters living at the park each summer day, greeting guests, posing for pictures, and making everyone's visit more enjoyable—for some, even unforgettable.

Take, for example, the young girl in a wheelchair, who had "Happy Birthday" sung to her by Snow White and the Seven Dwarfs. Or the lost little boy comforted by Goofy until his parents found him at the Lost Children's Station. Or the foreign child who learned, to his delight, that all of the Characters could speak to him in the universal language of laughter.

To them, and to thousands of other Disneyland guests, meeting the Characters in the park is as much a thrill as riding the Matterhorn or sailing the seas with the Pirates of the Caribbean.

For adults, too, there is something magical about really meeting make-believe heroes of half-forgotten fairy tales, seeing a live version of a long-ago storybook illustration, or hugging a childhood doll come-to-life.

All of the Disneyland Characters are warm and friendly, even Grumpy and evil Captain Hook, who manage to be loveable despite themselves. Guests

> "Until a character becomes a personality it cannot be believed. Without personality, the character may do funny or interesting things, but unless people are able to identify themselves with the character, its actions will seem unreal."
>
> —*Walt Disney*

flock to them as quickly as they run to Brer Fox or Pinocchio.

People of all ages find it a very special thrill to shake hands with the White Rabbit or see a child laugh as Dopey and Sneezy clown in front of Sleeping Beauty Castle. . . .

Drawing crowds every time and everywhere they appear, the Characters are likely to spend their time signing autographs or returning heartfelt hugs.

They can be found in their appropriate areas, many of them in Fantasyland. Brer Bear and Brer Fox (seen in *Song of the South*) hang out in New Orleans Square. Baloo and King Louie (of *The Jungle Book*) can be found in Adventureland, and so on. Most of the time, Mickey Mouse, Minnie, Donald Duck, Pluto, and Goofy are at the entrance to Main Street, U.S.A., where they cheerfully greet incoming guests and pose for pictures.

Literally millions of photographs are taken each year of Mickey Mouse, Prince John, Chip 'n' Dale, Mr. Smee, the Big Bad Wolf, and all their friends. And the characters try very hard to be sure that each guest gets a turn to snap the shutter for that once-in-a-lifetime photo of a family member with a family favorite . . .

Three members of the Disneyland population—Peter Pan, Snow White, and Alice (of Wonderland)—are the only three Characters who actually speak to the guests, although many of the other Characters can't resist asking a toddler her name or passing along a quick "hello" with a handshake.

Although summer sees some forty different Characters mixing it up with guests, they represent only the most famous of the Disney creations. Disneyland's Costume Department has hundreds of other costumes in storage. Virtually every cartoon character to

appear in a Disney movie is represented—from one of the geese in *The Aristocats* to a mushroom from *Fantasia*. Many of the costumes were first used in the "Fantasy on Parade" presentation a few years ago, but are seldom used now.

Walt Disney himself conceived the idea of using the Characters at Disneyland. He felt that it would be a great way to bring his screen classics to life, to give thousands of guests who visit the park each day the unforgettable thrill of meeting Mickey Mouse, Donald Duck, and all the other Characters who populate the world of imagination.

It takes only one look at a child's happy face to know that Walt Disney was right. ∎

◀◀ Like with so many Hollywood celebrities, the Disney Characters' appearances may vary over the years, but their personalities remain timeless.

Celebration is a constant at *Disneyland* Park; every year events and festivities mark national holidays, Character birthdays, and anniversaries of the Park itself.

"He was concerned that everyone be happy.
He had a passion for people being happy."

—*Mary Costa, voice of Sleeping Beauty*

Long a treasured
souvenir of a
Disneyland Park visit,
the Mickey Mouse
balloon is now
eco-friendly.

BUILDING THE PERFECT RACE CAR

From *Disney News*, Fall 1978

The idea of a perfect car seems like a wonderful, impossible dream for the next century. But several years ago, a group of designers created a small-scale race car that, for all practical purposes, is indestructible. With scheduled maintenance and minor repair, the car should last forever.

This vehicle of the future is found today, appropriately enough, in Tomorrowland at the Autopia in Disneyland and at the Grand Prix Raceway in the Walt Disney World Magic Kingdom. But the sleek, fiberglass race car that carries passengers around the winding courses is a far cry from the first Autopia cars created for Disneyland in 1954. At the end of their first day of operation, many of the new cars were too worn to run anymore; they literally fell apart.

Following that day, the designers at MAPO (the Disney organization in California responsible for the engineering and installation of new products) began a test program to create a new type of car, one that could survive a daily diet of sixteen hours in motion in low gear and a hundred rear-end collisions.

By the 1960s, the MAPO team had developed a car with a three-to-four year lifespan. But they still weren't satisfied. They didn't want a car that ran a few years; they wanted a car that would last forever. Finally in 1967, they incorporated everything they'd learned from six earlier prototypes with two new concepts. The result was the Mark VII design, and it worked.

The key to its success lies in the frame. Explains Bob Gurr, the director of special vehicle development at MAPO, "We finally designed a frame that would withstand those 300 crashes a day without breaking. Where the metal parts in the other car models were simply welded together (and often broke apart), the Mark VII frame is flexible and resilient, so it gives under pressure."

"The other important principle we discovered," Bob continues, "was to avoid any cantilevered loads (extended structures) on the welded parts. If everything is supported, it will all be strong."

When constructed in 1967, each car had a price tag identical to that of a full-size luxury car. Ten years later, most of those cars are showing their age, while the Disney racers are still going strong. Now, once a year, instead of going to a junkyard, the race cars go to the Disney facilities shops for basic repairs and part replacements. On a rotating schedule, every car goes into the shop to be taken apart and stripped to its frame. Each part, including the brakes, clutch, bearings, and so on, is checked for wear and then replaced or rebuilt.

Not surprisingly, the clutches in the little cars receive more abuse than almost any other part. Problem after problem occurred, but no clutch could be found that would hold up to the grueling pace of the cars. So in 1968, Gurr decided:

"Let's invent our own!" They did, adapting the model successfully into all the race cars—with no more problems.

The yearly checkups include more than a look under the hood; careful attention also is given to the cars' fiberglass exteriors. Each is rubbed down, given necessary repairs, and repainted. Because of its ability to withstand high-impact crashes without breaking, fiberglass was chosen to replace the metal bodies of earlier models. If damage does occur, an easily repaired crack instead of a dent is the result.

While the MAPO designers were overcoming mechanical and structural problems, they also had to contend with the difficulties the small-size vehicles presented in designing a functional yet sporty-looking car.

"The problem," Gurr relates, "was to make a little car that would hold big people." Their solution was to design a long front hood that was lower than the fend-

ers, to create an illusion of sleekness. Adults could stretch their legs, while the car still looked stylish—much like a popular, full-size sports car. The chopped-off Kamm back was adopted for the rear of the car where the engine is placed.

Since children as well as adults sit behind the wheels of the racers, the cars must be easy to drive. A single foot pedal acts as both the accelerator and brake (push it down and the car goes up to seven m.p.h.; let it up and it slows to a stop). Even people who have never driven before can handle these racers easily. In fact, a Disney race car is often the first car a person learns to drive. . . .

The race cars that crossed the finish line for the first time a decade ago are the same ones in operation at Disneyland and the Walt Disney World Magic Kingdom today. Thousands of miles later, they still look and drive like new cars, and are expected to do so for many more years. And that comes close to just about everybody's idea of a perfect car. ■

Autopia **is the only existing** *Tomorrowland* **Area attraction dating all the way back to Opening Day, July 17, 1955.**

The 1970s saw
several major pre-
mieres at *Disneyland
Park: Big Thunder
Mountain Railroad*
Attraction became
the wildest ride in
the wilderness, *Space
Mountain* Attraction
took flight in a
refreshed *Tomorrow-
land* Area, and the
renovated *Matter-
horn Bobsleds*
Attraction became
home to an abom-
inable new tenant.

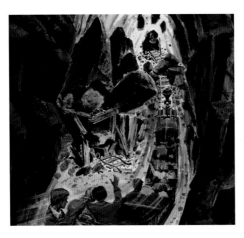

COSTUMING A CAST OF THOUSANDS

From *Disney News*, Fall 1979

Although many of the performers on the Disney stage are Audio-Animatronics Figures going through their paces unerringly, the most-applauded members of the cast are not made of computerized circuits and intricate mechanical workings, but rather flesh and blood. On an average day, for instance, a . . . guest may come into contact with more than fifteen hosts and hostesses before ever setting foot inside the Magic Kingdom, and once his day is over, he may have personally met over seventy-five cast members—serving food, answering questions, staffing attractions, or performing countless other on-stage roles. And just like the architecture, landscaping, entertainment, and interior design, employees must be compatible with the essence of each area . . .

Whether the costume brings to life a character from a Disney movie, recreates a mood from the past, or suggests a look for the future, the vital ingredient is not necessarily realism, but a blending of the real and the imaginary . . .

Besides the task of maintaining a working wardrobe . . . the Costume Division is also responsible for costumes for parades, special events, live entertainment groups, the Walt Disney Characters, and more than one thousand special garments donned by Audio-Animatronics Figures in many of the Magic Kingdom attractions.

"It's a Small World" features more than 600 figures in native dress from every section of the globe. In fact, Disney costume designers traveled 25,000 miles gathering fabric and accessories for the show. . . . The Costume Division's role in the continually developing Disney show includes researching, designing, and producing new costumes, redesigning and updating existing costumes, as well as daily laundering, dry-cleaning, and repairing so that every item—basic garments, shoes, hats, ties, belts, scarves, spats, cuff links, and riding crops—is clean and ready to go at a moment's notice.

Although costuming the cast is just one ingredient in the overall themed show, it plays a vitally important role in helping to create the mood. Whether a steamboat captain, a Polynesian . . . hostess or a monorail pilot, each cast member is assigned a specially designed wardrobe to complement the total scene. ■

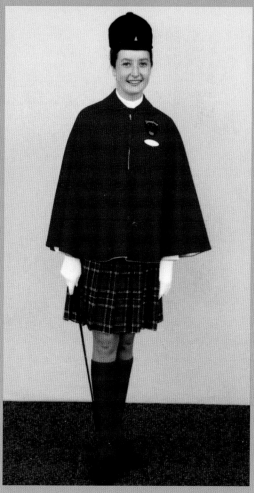

The beloved characters of Disney films have a home in many of the attractions and much of the entertainment at *Disneyland* Park.

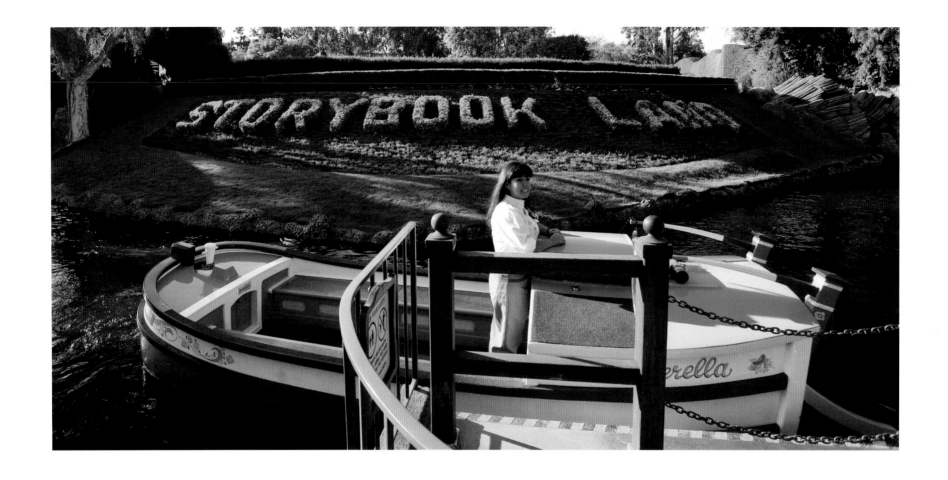

"It's just been sort of a dress rehearsal, and we're just getting started. So if any of you start resting on your laurels, I mean just forget it, because … we are just getting started."

—*Walt Disney*

Menacing Monstro ▶▶
the Whale perpetually
gives the "fish eye"
to passersby.

Eighties Explosion

Change upon change—the constancy and vitality of change was the rhythm of the fourth decade of *Disneyland* Park.

Around the world, there was general, social, economic, and political upheaval as wealth, business, and Western culture in general began to migrate to new industrializing economies. Words such as "globalization" and "multinational" began entering the common vernacular, and major corporations and industries relocated in Eastern Europe following the collapse of communism, and into new market economies in Mexico, Korea, and China.

The Walt Disney Company was involved in upheavals of its own during the period. A brutal, hostile takeover attempt and drastic management shift shook the Company to its foundations, and for a time left its future in serious doubt. Fans worldwide kept vigilant watch, and worried that their beloved Disney would be broken apart and sold for its assets.

Fortunately, the new management led by Michael Eisner and Frank Wells, as well as Studio head Jeffrey Katzenberg, carried on the innovations begun at Disney in the early 1980s, and leveraged the global embrace of the Disney culture to more aggressively mine potential applications of the Disney name and business model to new areas of entertainment, retail, and leisure.

Disney's revenues soon began to grow, improving approximately twenty percent annually during the second half of the 1980s. Disney moved from last place to first place in motion picture revenues among the eight major studios—but the Parks and Resorts were still responsible for about seventy percent of the Company's revenue.

Disneyland Resort Paris opened in Marne-la-Vallée, outside of Paris on April 12, 1992; and *Tokyo Disneyland* Resort continued to expand, regularly attracting extraordinary crowds.

Although seemingly always in danger of being supplanted by new technology such as the quickly evolving video games, or new entertainment

A simple scenic space tour departing for the forest Moon of Endor and those lovable Ewoks—what can possibly go wrong?

One of the biggest attraction debuts of the 1980s was celebrated with a spectacular opening party.

media such as home entertainment (or falling attendance that was conventionally predicted as the result of the opening of other Disney parks around the world), *Disneyland* Park continued to prove, time and again, that its guest experience could outshine any other entertainment form—even competition from other "Magic Kingdoms."

An "extreme makeover" of Mickey's longtime gal pal was part of a huge 1986 Company-wide initiative including a television special and a daily *Disneyland* Park parade and event, "Totally Minnie." Themed events and new parades kept a refreshed and revitalized *Disneyland* Park in the news and in the popular forefront. These new draws included Circus Fantasy, Snow White's 50th Anniversary, State Fair, Blast to the Past, Mickey is 60, Party Gras, The World According to Goofy, Aladdin's Royal Caravan, and The Lion King Celebration.

The 1990 celebration of the thirty-fifth anniversary of *Disneyland* Park reunited the "Dateline: Disneyland" Opening Day television hosts Bob Cummings, Art Linkletter, and former President Ronald Reagan.

The Disney Imagineers and their colleagues kept the Park fresh by reaching out to entertainment allies such as George Lucas, resulting in the 3D multimedia spectacular *Captain EO* and

the groundbreaking interstellar adventure *Star Tours* Attraction.

In the midst of the hue and cry of die-hard Disney fans that these innovative attractions were not "Disney," a pioneering log flume experience, *Splash Mountain* Attraction, was developed around the adventures of Brer Fox and Brer Bear in pursuit of mischievous Brer Rabbit from the 1946 Disney classic *Song of the South*.

In addition, the ambitious all-new themed *Mickey's Toontown* Area, based on the beloved classic Characters and new favorites from Disney's latest television animation, was developed and premiered in 1993.

A spectacular nighttime fireworks and "visual hydrotechnic" extravaganza on the Rivers of America, the *Fantasmic!* show brought together Disneyland Entertainment, Walt Disney Feature Animation, and Walt Disney Imagineering in one of the most dazzling and original shows ever presented.

Always bringing Guests something new, the excitement of innovation, thrilling and inventive events and spectaculars, and the enduring traditions of generations past made *Disneyland* Park a fashionable destination again, and the exclamation, "I'm going to Disneyland!" became a national motto. ◼

Splash Mountain
Attraction opened
on July 17, 1989.
It has a flume length
of 2,640 feet (804.7
meters), 103 Audio-
Animatronics Figures,
and a forty-five-
degree drop from
Chickapin Hill into
the Briar Patch.

NEW HORIZONS

Excerpt from *Disneyland: Inside Story*, 1987

By Randy Bright

"The way I see it," Walt Disney often said, "Disneyland will never be finished. It's something we can keep developing and adding to."

In the more than two decades since his passing, not only did Disneyland continue to grow and flourish, but the theme park also moved to Florida in the form of Walt Disney World's Magic Kingdom, traveled across the Pacific Ocean as Tokyo Disneyland, and went back to Florida with the creation of EPCOT Center. Today, with four major theme parks in operation and another on the horizon in Europe, one might assume that Disneyland, the original, could be somewhat overshadowed in the future.

"Not so," says Disney's Michael Eisner. "Disneyland remains the flagship," he maintains, "the experimental place to do things that could translate to our other parks. To keep Disneyland on the leading edge, we'll be constantly looking at new ways to combine art and technology, just as Disney has always done. But the main emphasis will remain—that we're there to entertain and be creative and fanciful, while we look to the brighter side of things."

Looking to the brighter side of things has certainly been the trademark of Disneyland since its very beginning. "When you react to things, you're alive," says John Hench, reflecting on his half-century career at Disney. "I think people in Disneyland react and expand very easily. Unlike in society's modern cities, they can drop their defenses in Disneyland and look other people in the eye. Actually, what we're selling throughout the Park is reassurance. We offer adventures in which you survive a kind of personal challenge—a charging hippo, a runaway mine train, a wicked witch, an out-of-control bobsled. But in every case, we let you win. We let your survival instincts triumph over adversity. A trip to Disneyland is an exercise in reassurance about oneself and one's ability to maybe even handle the real challenges in life."

Designer Tony Baxter speaks for the new Walt Disney Imagineering generation that grew up on the reassurance that Hench helped to create. "I don't ever ask myself if Walt would like this or that," he says. "Most of us today have been around Disney since we were kids. If we don't have a feeling for what it means now, we wouldn't be here. When we work on a project, we really have everybody put their feelings into it. That's our best assurance for future success." ■

DISNEYLAND'S 35TH ANNIVERSARY

By Tim O'Day

Deep in the DNA of *Disneyland* Park is an apparent desire to commemorate the Park's major milestone anniversaries. This probably stems from the fact that *Disneyland* Park was never expected to survive and prosper. Obviously, *Disneyland* Park has endured, and as the first decade of the twenty-first century draws to a close, the Park has welcomed well over 500 million guests from every point on the globe.

Through the years, the Park's anniversary celebrations have taken various forms. In 1965, the "Tencennial" celebration marked the Park's first decade while the theme of "Twenty-fifth Family Reunion" provided the background for the Park's silver anniversary in 1980.

On the morning of January 11, 1990, Disney executives Michael D. Eisner, Frank Wells, and Roy E. Disney were joined on the steps of the Main Street Train Station by an impressive trio of Disneyland Opening Day alumni: former U.S. President Ronald Reagan (fresh from two terms in the White House) and legendary TV stars Art Linkletter and Bob Cummings. Along with Walt Disney, Reagan, Linkletter, and

Cummings had hosted the grand opening of *Disneyland* Park via a live national television broadcast on July 17, 1955.

Now, nearly thirty-five years later, the trio reunited in an unprecedented re-dedication of the Park and the official kick-off of a yearlong thirty-fifth anniversary celebration. During his remarks, President Reagan commented: "It is an honor and a privilege to join with you as we re-dedicate one of America's national treasures . . . a place that has captured the imagination and earned the affection of four generations of Americans . . . a place that has served as host and goodwill ambassador to millions of visitors from abroad."

The Park's thirty-fifth anniversary was celebrated in grand style with the premiere of the "Party Gras Parade," a most unique approach to anniversary festivities. Filled with wild Latin rhythms, conga lines, fruity headdresses, colorful costumes, stilt-walkers, showers of confetti, and six thirty-seven-foot-tall Disney Character inflatable balloon floats that towered over *Main Street, U.S.A.* Area, it was less a parade and more a gigantic moving musical pro-

duction number that stopped at pre-set intervals to fully engage the audience. It was not easy to resist the fun and energy of the entire spectacle.

Following the re-dedication ceremony and his participation in the parade, President Reagan went backstage to personally meet and greet the performers, congratulating them on an outstanding inaugural performance. A *Disneyland* Park staff photographer happened to catch the moment as the fortieth president of the United States mingled with Conga dancers, tastefully attired showgirls, and stunt performers, and marveled at the giant balloons.

A highlight of the year was the tour of Mickey's Mouseorail across North America, visiting twenty-five cities in the United States and Canada. The trip was made in a one-of-a-kind bright-red vehicle that was rebuilt and converted from the last of the Mark III *Disneyland* Park Monorail trains that circled the Park from 1969 to 1988. Imagine driving through your hometown and encountering what appears to be a classic *Disneyland* Park Monorail navigating down the street with Mickey Mouse at the helm! ■

A CAREFREE REALM

Excerpt from
Disneyland: Inside Story, 1987

By Michael Eisner, former chairman,
The Walt Disney Company

Like most youngsters in the post–World War II years, I grew up watching Mickey and Donald and Brer Fox and *The Wonderful World of Disney*.

But Disneyland was an impossible dream. In those days, thirteen-year-old New York kids didn't travel cross-country to live out their fantasies, not even in the world's greatest theme park.

Years later, as tourists, my wife, Jane, and I finally entered the gates of the Magic Kingdom. Whatever youthful images I'd once conjured up were dwarfed by the beauty and spectacle of the place. The reality was better than the illusion.

That was almost twenty years ago. Sad to say, I'm no longer often able to look at Disneyland through the eyes of a visitor. The park that once was solely my pleasure is now part of my job.

Today there are other, newer Disney parks—in Florida, in Japan, and, soon in France—but Disneyland remains our flagship. Everything we've built since 1955 is a reflection of its creative spirit. Most of our best new ideas still get their start in the original Magic Kingdom.

On that first, long-ago visit, Jane and I stepped from the chill and gloom of an Eastern winter into the sunny glow of Main Street, a place so clean that it seemed we could eat right off the sidewalk, a place where our cares and concerns somehow couldn't get past the gate. ∎

The varied crafts and disciplines of the Imagineers are seen here. "We're always exploring and experimenting," Walt Disney said. "We call it Imagineering—the blending of creative imagination with technical know-how."

"Imagineering is the first stage," Walt said. "Engineering the second, and then construction and installing the exhibits . . . so there's never a dull moment, you might say!"

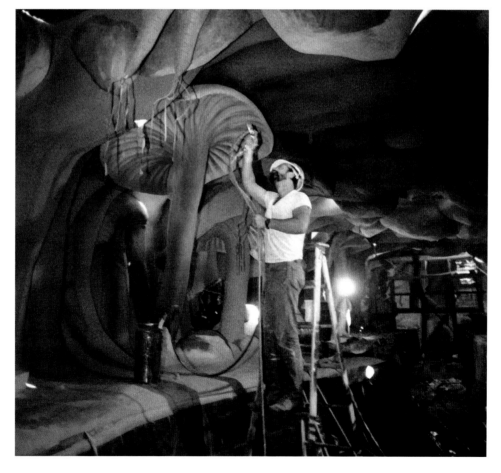

Disneyland Park reaches a healthy "forty years young" without a midlife crisis, and with a "middle-aged spread" that was intentional, carefully designed, and planned by the Imagineers.

WALLY BOAG

From *Disney News*,
Summer 1990

Wally Boag, known to Disneyland guests for twenty-seven years as the adroit comic star of the Golden Horseshoe Revue, clearly loved his creative tenure with Walt Disney. . . .

Boag was a stage performer for twenty-two of his thirty-four years when he signed a two-week contract to appear in Disneyland's Golden Horseshoe Revue, a rollicking frontier stage show featuring music, dancing, and comedy. He generated laughs as both a brash traveling salesman—complete with a rubber chicken and maneuverable toupee—and gun-toting cowboy Pecos Bill since the Park's opening day in 1955.

He did it so well he stayed until 1982, retiring after 40,000 performances, assuring his place in *The Guinness Book of World Records*.

Boag's delight with his Disney days was not one-sided. "Walt loved the Golden Horseshoe," he recalls. "The stage-left box was designated as his. He often brought guests to see the show, and one time he brought in the Frontierland Indian performers—in complete war-dance regalia!" Boag remembers this well, as he got a big laugh out of Walt when he ripped off his toupee, handed it to Chief Whitehorse, and said, "Here, take this. I'll save you the trouble!"

But Walt relied on Boag for more than his vaudevillian antics; he asked him to join the Imagineers at Walt Disney Imagineering (at that time, WED) to help develop the *Haunted Mansion* and *Enchanted Tiki Room* for Disneyland. Boag not only wrote a significant portion of the *Tiki Room* show but provided the voices for some of the fledgling *Audio-Animatronics* birds including José, the avian emcee. "It was wonderful to have a boss whose calls often meant yet another creative opportunity," he says.

"The last time I saw Walt was about two weeks before he died. It was when they were building Club 33 (a private dining room in Disneyland) and Walt and Roy's suite in New Orleans Square. I was over at the construction site and there was Walt and Mrs. Disney and their two grandchildren.

"He said, 'This is going to be great. We're going to use all the furniture from *The Happiest Millionaire*. That picture didn't make a lot of money, so we're going to get some use out of it.'

"I had to get back to the show, so I left them, and I never saw him again."

Boag still finds time to perform between gardening and golf, making an occasional appearance on television and commuting from Southern California a few times a year to appear at Las Vegas conventions.

Clearly, his association with Walt transcended a business relationship. "His mind was brilliant," he says, "and all of a sudden, he was gone. There's so much more I'd like to have talked to him about." ■

The denizens of ▶▶ Disney's animated shorts have their own hometown at *Disneyland* Park, in *Mickey's Toontown* Area. Visitors can meet Mickey, Minnie, Donald, and Goofy, and take a wild ride in Lenny the Cab. There's a comic reality at work here, and a straight line or a right angle are rare in this cartoon come to life.

"You can't live on things made for children or for critics. I've never made films for either of them. Disneyland is not just for children. I don't play down."
—*Walt Disney*

1995–2005

The Millennium Approaches

As the 1990s came to a close, worldwide anticipation of the closing of the second millennium, and the end of the twentieth century, inspired countless New Year's Eve celebrations on December 31, 1999, welcoming the year 2000.

In the United States, an aggressive economic growth continued. Personal incomes increased dramatically after the recession of 1990, and there was higher productivity overall.

Technology that would have amazed even a buff like Walt Disney became reality. Computer hardware and software continued to progress—and to transform the popular culture with advances in video gaming, music delivery systems, and video transmission formats.

Disneyland Park celebrated "40 Years of Adventure" with the opening of the *Indiana Jones*™ Adventure: Temple of the Forbidden Eye Attraction, a creative collaboration of Disney and George Lucas. Based on the blockbuster *Indiana Jones*™ films, modified military transport

vehicles convey passengers through a lost temple with Indiana Jones™ in order to discover the secrets of the goddess Mara. More than 400 Imagineers worked on its design and construction, with a core team of nearly one hundred, led by show producer Tony Baxter. The *Jungle Cruise* Attraction was rerouted to provide better access to the experience, and a half-mile-long queue area led to a gigantic 50,000-square-foot interior show building.

The theme of adventure continued later in the decade, when Edgar Rice Burroughs' famed ape man (as interpreted by Disney animators) evicted the Swiss Family Robinson in order to become the landlord of the jungle in Tarzan's Treehouse™ Attraction. *Tomorrowland* Area underwent significant growing pains during this period, with the opening (and swift closing) of *Rocket Rods*, an innovative ride system that was just a little too far in the future for daily operation. An exhibit highlighting space exploration in conjunction with NASA's fortieth anniversary, The American Space Experience was a favorite, and *Honey,*

◀◀ The animated roots of the Disney Studio are celebrated and demonstrated in *The Art of Disney Animation* Attraction at *Disney's California Adventure* Park.

The *Astro Orbiter* Attraction is the most recent in a line of spaceship-spinning pylon monument attractions at *Disneyland* Park, including the Astro-Jets (1956–1964), Tomorrowland Jets (1964–1966), and Rocket Jets (1967–1997).

I Shrunk the Audience Attraction, a popular 3D film with elaborate in-theatre effects, opened.

In keeping with a tradition established by Walt Disney of showcasing cutting-edge and inspiring ideas within *Tomorrowland* Area, *Innoventions* Entertainment Facility served as a kind of futuristic trade show, displaying cutting-edge technologies for consumers, industrial, and business applications.

Adventures of a gentler kind were available in *Critter Country* Area as with the opening of *The Many Adventures of Winnie the Pooh* Attraction, a beehive-based journey through the Hundred Acre Wood with Eeyore, Kanga and little Roo, Rabbit, Piglet, Owl, but most of all Winnie the Pooh.

In the late 1990s, the planning and Imagineering began to expand *Disneyland* Park from a single-park, one-hotel property into an ambitious vacation resort development.

The key components of this resort were a second theme park, *Disney's California Adventure* Park, constructed on the site of the original *Disneyland* Park parking lot. Because of this, the first project in the resort expansion was the six-level 10,250-space "Mickey and Friends" parking structure. At the time of its completion in 2000, it was the largest parking structure in the United States.

The fifty-five-acre *Disney's California Adventure* Park consisted of five areas: *Sunshine Plaza* Area, *Hollywood Pictures Backlot* Area, *The Golden State* Area, *A Bug's Land* Area, and *Paradise Pier* Area, each evoking aspects of California, its culture, landmarks, and history.

The *Disneyland* Hotel was also extensively renovated and remodeled, and a spectacular new resort hotel, *Disney's Grand Californian* Hotel & Spa, was constructed. *The Pan Pacific Hotel* was also extensively improved and renamed *Disney's Pacific Hotel* and then *Disney's Paradise Pier Hotel*.

Between the hotels and the theme parks was built a kinetic shopping, dining, and entertainment complex called *Downtown Disney* District, offering something for everyone. While many young people enjoyed its visceral nightlife feel, *Downtown Disney* District also offered a twelve-screen movie theater, family-oriented dining such as the Rainforest Café, and one of the largest Disney shopping experiences on Earth, at the World of Disney Store.

As the twentieth century closed and the new millennium began, *Disneyland* Resort not only retained its relevance, it began a whole new generation of leisure experiences and entertainment traditions designed to carry it into future decades. ■

Disney's Grand Californian Hotel & Spa combines the majesty of the grand hotels of days gone by with the warm and intimate décor of an Arts and Crafts-style living room.

ENDURING IMPORTANCE

Excerpted from the introduction of
Disneyland: Then, Now, and Forever, 2005

By Julie Andrews

One memory I'll cherish forever is the thrill of seeing Disneyland for the first time. And guess who my tour guide was? Walt Disney! People just stopped and stared at him, they couldn't believe it was him. They recognized him, they reached out their hands to touch him—they were absolutely beaming and so was he—and so was I.

I have been to Disneyland many times since with my children, and now my grandchildren, but nothing will top that moment. It seemed you could see the whole park reflected in his eyes, his dream had come true. A dream that we could all share—and we did, we do, and we shall as long as there is a child left in each of us.

Disneyland was Walt's gift to a weary world. Once you pass through its gates, the stress and strife of our everyday reality seems to melt away, and we enter a truly timeless realm that has withstood trends and fads to become a national treasure. Most importantly though, over the past fifty years, more than six generations of family and friends from all over the world have gathered together in this happy place to experience its special brand of magic and the gifts of laughter, fun, nostalgia, fantasy, and adventure.

When Walt declared on Opening Day that "Disneyland is your land," I'm not sure if he truly realized how people everywhere would embrace the Park as their own. No other form of entertainment is as universally beloved and cherished as Disneyland by people of all ages, backgrounds, and origins.

As people come to Disneyland during its Happiest Homecoming on Earth celebration to mark its fiftieth anniversary, they will experience a park that is as vibrant and relevant today as it was in 1955. Disneyland is fifty years young and yet ageless. ∎

British film and stage actress, singer, and author Julie Andrews made her movie debut in the title role of Walt Disney's *Mary Poppins,* for which she won the Academy Award® for best actress. In 2000, she was made a Dame Commander of the British Empire (DBE). From 2005 to 2006, Andrews served as the Honorary Homecoming Ambassador for the *Disneyland* Park 50th anniversary celebration, Happiest Homecoming on Earth, traveling to promote the celebration and appearing at several events at the Resort.

On October 5, 2004, America's three most celebrated swimmers—Michael Phelps, Ian Crocker, and Lenny Krayzelburg—swam down *Main Street, U.S.A.* Area in a specially constructed Olympic-length pool (which took thirty hours to build).

Familiar faces of *Disneyland* Park. How many of these memorable mugs can you find in the Magic Kingdom?

Paradise Pier Area is a loving tribute to seaside boardwalks and amusement piers that offered inexpensive entertainment and fresh air as an escape from the crowded urban centers of the early twentieth century.

THE HAPPIEST CELEBRATION ON EARTH

By Tim O'Day

Anticipation. Excitement. Fun. Emotion. Charm. Nostalgia. Pride. These are just a few of the words that could describe the feelings guests experienced in 2005 and 2006 during the fiftieth anniversary of *Disneyland* Resort. The eighteen-month-long worldwide Happiest Celebration on Earth paid tribute to Walt Disney's original dream of *Disneyland* Park.

Walt Disney's original Magic Kingdom was feted in grand style like never before. Sleeping Beauty Castle, the Park's iconic centerpiece, was transformed into a sparkling jewel just for the occasion—highlighted by five golden "crowns"—one for each decade.

Remember... Dreams Come True Fireworks Spectacular used the skies over the castle to tell the Park's amazing story through never-before-seen pyrotechnics, an incredible soundtrack comprised of fifty years of familiar *Disneyland* Park music, and an all-new flight path for Tinker Bell! On *Main Street, U.S.A.* Area, Walt Disney's Parade of Dreams dazzled audiences with one of the most elaborate parade productions ever staged at *Disneyland* Park. Featuring one of the largest casts of Disney Characters and performers ever assembled, along with Audio-Animatronics Figures, waterfalls, jumping fountains, wafting bubbles, and acrobatic performers, the parade was a fitting tribute to the world of Disney imagination.

New attractions were also unveiled during the anniversary festivities. *Buzz Lightyear Astro Blasters* Attraction became the first Disney Park attraction in the world to meld an on-board experience with real-time online interactivity. *Space Mountain* Attraction re-opened as a re-Imagineered twenty-first century thrill adventure, rededicated by none other than legendary U.S. Astronaut Neil Armstrong. On *Main Street, U.S.A.* Area, Donald Duck attempted to host the new film *Disneyland: The First 50 Magical Years* featuring former *Disneyland* Cast Member (and Hollywood film star) Steve Martin.

Across the esplanade at *Disney's California Adventure* Park, the high-energy musical extravaganza *Block Party Bash*, featuring characters from all of the Disney/Pixar films, had guests groovin' in the streets. Audience interactivity was also taken to a new level with the debut of *Turtle Talk with Crush* Attraction, part of the Disney Animation exhibit in the Park's *Hollywood Pictures Backlot* Area.

Throughout The Happiest Celebration on Earth (a nod to the familiar *Disneyland* Resort descriptor—The Happiest Place on Earth), the Park was honored with numerous accolades and honors. *Disneyland* Resort became the first non-celebrity to be honored by the Hollywood Walk of Fame. It was saluted with an evening of music at the world-famous Hollywood Bowl, and a *Mad Tea Party* Attraction cup and familiar *Dumbo The Flying Elephant* Attraction vehicle were inducted into the Smithsonian Institution recognizing the Park's significant place in American pop culture.

Lastly, the 2005 National Thanksgiving Turkey, named Marshmallow, put *Disneyland* Resort in headlines around the world. Following the traditional "pardon" ceremony at the White House (sparing the bird from being Thanksgiving dinner at the famous residence), Marshmallow had a police escort to the airport where he flew west (on an airplane, first-class, 2,288 miles non-stop) to become The Happiest Turkey on Earth and another memorable participant in The Happiest Celebration on Earth. ■

Elegant but ominous, the Hollywood Tower Hotel looms over unsuspecting visitors who might hazard its decaying splendor in an endeavor to solve the mysteries within *The Twilight Zone Tower of Terror* Attraction.

Passengers ride
along on a thrilling
excursion through
Monstropolis in
*Monsters, Inc.
Mike & Sulley to the
Rescue!* Attraction.

◀ Disney Animation
offers interactive
adventures—such as
Animation Academy,
Sorcerer's Workshop,
and *Turtle Talk with
Crush* Attraction—
that celebrate this
fantastic art form.

Sunshine Plaza Area offers welcome to Disney's celebration of the Golden State, featuring a giant stylized sun sheathed in brilliant titanium. Flower-shaped computer-programmed moving heliostats reflect the sun's light onto the faces of the sculpture, creating a live kinetic illumination.

2005–Present

Today to Tomorrow

The sixth decade of *Disneyland* Resort began with an invitation to come home. The first five decades of *Disneyland* Resort had created a multi-generational global family numbering into the millions. In honor of that home and that family, an eighteen-month-long celebration (May 5, 2005 through September 30, 2006) of the fiftieth anniversary of *Disneyland* Resort was celebrated—The Happiest Homecoming on Earth.

The Happiest Homecoming on Earth ceremony began with a dedication from then-Disney CEO Michael Eisner, and included fireworks, remarks from Julie Andrews (Honorary Homecoming Ambassador for the fiftieth anniversary celebrations) and Art Linkletter (original TV anchor for the Opening Day broadcast); a performance of the Disney theme "When You Wish Upon A Star" by pop star (and former Mouseketeer) Christina Aguilera; and LeAnn Rimes singing the fiftieth anniversary theme song, "Remember When," composed by Richard Marx.

Many classic *Disneyland* Park attractions—such as Walt Disney's Enchanted Tiki Room, the *Jungle Cruise* Attraction, and *Space Mountain* Attraction—re-opened in 2005 after special refurbishments. Other refurbishments have taken place around *Disneyland* Resort with many areas being repainted and restored to their former glory. *Tomorrowland* Area, *Main Street, U.S.A.* Area, and Sleeping Beauty Castle were all given special exterior color treatments, and the castle was specially decorated for the celebration.

The original attractions that opened with the Park each had a ride vehicle painted gold (fifty years traditionally being the Golden Anniversary), and the Park also contained fifty Hidden Mickeys—golden Mickey Mouse heads with "50" displayed in the middle.

A new fireworks show, Remember … Dreams Come True Fireworks Spectacular premiered, and Walt Disney's Parade of Dreams featured elaborate floats with lighting that allowed for both daytime and nighttime performances.

◄◄ The new attracting icon of the *Disney's California Adventure* Park entry sequence is the lost, lamented Beverly Hills Carthay Circle Theater (1926–1969), which hosted the 1937 premiere of Walt Disney's *Snow White and the Seven Dwarfs* and the 1940 roadshow engagement of Walt Disney's *Fantasia*.

Former *Disneyland* Park Cast Member, actor-playwright, and author Steve Martin opened *Disneyland: The First 50 Magical Years* Exhibition, which featured a film starring Martin . . . and Donald Duck.

Pixar became more fully entwined in the *Disneyland* Resort culture with the addition of *Buzz Lightyear Astro Blasters* Attraction (featuring the characters from Disney/Pixar's *Toy Story 2*), *Finding Nemo Submarine Voyage* Attraction starring the characters of Disney/Pixar's *Finding Nemo*, and *Toy Story Midway Mania* Attraction at *Disney's California Adventure* Park.

The *Block Party Bash* also premiered. A "mobile stage show" rather than a typical parade, *Block Party Bash* was inspired by the Pixar films: *Toy Story*, *A Bug's Life*, *Monsters, Inc.*, and *The Incredibles*. In addition to the characters, *Block Party Bash* featured a huge cadre of sixty dancers, sixteen acrobats, thirty bikers, twelve pairs of jumping stilts, and even trampoline artists!

The Pixar Play Parade premiered later, as did

parades and entertainment featuring music and characters from Disney's phenomenal *High School Musical* films including shows such as *High School Musical Pep Rally*, *High School Musical 2: School's Out!* and *High School Musical 3: Now or Never*.

In October 2007, The Walt Disney Company unveiled a significant multi-year expansion plan for the *Disneyland* Resort to continue its growth as a multi-day, world-class tourist destination.

Announced by Disney President and Chief Executive Officer Bob Iger and Parks and Resorts Chairman Jay Rasulo at a press conference at Walt Disney Imagineering's Glendale head-quarters, the expansion will bring new entertainment and major family-oriented attractions to *Disney's California Adventure* Park, including an entirely new *Cars Land* Area inspired by the hit Disney/Pixar animated film *Cars*.

"This plan is a reflection of our belief in the bright future of the Disneyland Resort and our continuing commitment to grow the Anaheim Resort Area as a world-class tourist destination," said Iger.

Icons of Golden State history and culture abound in *Disney's California Adventure* Park.

Disney Imagineers will be bringing more of Walt Disney into *Disney's California Adventure* Park, celebrating the hope and optimism of California that attracted Walt to this land of opportunity in the 1920s. Guests entering the new Plaza will be instantly immersed in the world that inspired Walt during his early days as an animation pioneer. The new, interactive *Walt Disney Story* Attraction will set the stage for the unfolding legacy of Walt that will permeate the park.

The expansive program reaches throughout *Disney's California Adventure* Park, with an amazing Little Mermaid attraction, a groundbreaking, signature nighttime spectacular with a new viewing area for 9,000, and the addition of the twelve-acre *Cars Land* Area featuring the world of Radiator Springs with three new attractions. Extensive landscaping and new retail and dining spots will create an even richer environment throughout the Park in ways that reinforce Guests' connection with Walt.

"Our Disneyland Resort Guests have a deep emotional connection with Walt Disney, whose life story really captures the pioneering spirit of California in the 1920s," said Rasulo. "The creative evolution of Disney's California Adventure Park will connect guests to Walt's own California adventure and reflect the place that he found when he first arrived with a cardboard suitcase in his hand and a head full of dreams."

In 1966, Walt Disney told KNBC reporter Bob Wright, "There's a little plaque out there that says: 'As long as there's imagination in the world Disneyland will never be complete.' So we have big plans . . .

"I think by this time my staff, my young group of executives, and everything else, are convinced that Walt is right. That quality will out. And so I think they're going to stay with that policy because it's proved that it's a good business policy.

"Give the people everything you can give them. Keep the place as clean as you can keep it. Keep it friendly, you know. Make it a real fun place to be. I think they're convinced and I think they'll hang on after as you say . . . well . . . after Disney." ■

Grizzly Peak and Roadside California programmatic architecture.

In most amusement
parks, the outdoors is
a "space between"
rides and shows. At
Disneyland Resort,
the outdoors is an
integral part of the
Guest experience,
filled with detail,
color, light—and
constant surprises.

Everywhere there are colorful musical events, ranging from intimate street performances to mobile spectaculars populated by dozens of individual set pieces and performers.

Disneyland Resort after dark has always had a busy, bright, and kinetic feeling, distinctly different from *Disneyland* Resort by day. *Downtown Disney* District carries on that tradition in its unique mix of dining, shopping, and activities.

Disneyland Park innovates in entertainment technology like fireworks. In 2004, compressed air launched the rockets skyward, replacing the noisier and dirtier black powder.

YOU CAN ALWAYS COME BACK TO *DISNEYLAND* PARK

By Tim O'Day

More than five decades have passed since the *Disneyland* Resort rose out of a Southern California orange grove and captured the imagination of generations from around the world—embraced as theirs by young and old alike. It is difficult, if not impossible, to imagine a world without *Disneyland* Park on the pop culture landscape. As famed author and futurist Ray Bradbury once said, "Disneyland liberates men to their better selves."

Of all the new forms of entertainment that have been produced since 1955, none has been so universally embraced as *Disneyland* Park. Its mere name has become so universally recognized that it has been used to introduce new audiences to the Disney experience in Japan, France, and China— all the while retaining its status as Disney's flagship Park and a uniquely American concept.

In 2005, the Smithsonian Institution's National Museum of American History recognized *Disneyland* Park as a national treasure by accessioning both a *Dumbo The Flying Elephant*

Attraction vehicle and a *Mad Tea Party* Attraction cup into their collection. *Disneyland* Park also became the first non-celebrity to be feted with a star on the Hollywood Walk of Fame.

Attracting people of every origin, *Disneyland* Park has played host to a veritable "Who's Who" during the past five decades. Seven U.S. presidents, countless foreign heads of state plus a constant parade of famed sports figures and entertainment celebrities have added to the Park's lore.

Walt Disney's "magical little park" has evolved to become a beloved and coveted destination, celebrated through the years in countless newspaper stories, magazine features, books, TV shows, scholarly museum exhibitions, and on numerous Web sites. It has been referenced in popular songs, films, and even a series of memorable commercials ("I'm going to Disneyland!").

According to cultural historian Karal Ann Marling, *Disneyland* Park is the "most complex, baffling, and beloved work of art produced in postwar America." It is a place built upon emotions and fond memo-

◄◄ A Walt Disney's Parade of Dreams float inspires magic and excitement for visitors young and young-at-heart.

The famous Pacific Electric Red Car rail line rides again, into a dream of Hollywood gone by.

ries. A first-time visit has become one of life's milestones, a treasured experiential tradition passed from one generation to the next.

What has secured the Park's place in world culture? It is the common bond of families and friends who have grown up with and experienced together the Park's special magic, making it a cherished part of our collective consciousness. It has withstood fads and trends to become a consistent source of joy and inspiration for every visitor. And unlike many other passages of life that cannot be relived, you can always come back to *Disneyland* Park.

The place that *Disneyland* Park holds in our society is indelible. Walt Disney himself touched the heart of his park's meaning when he said, "I think what I want Disneyland to be most of all is a happy place—a place where adults and children can experience together some of the wonders of life . . . and feel better because of it." ■

◄◄ A traditional Disney Fun Map shows the new and improved *Disney's California Adventure* Park.

Paradise Bay is home to the new nighttime Spectacular Walt Disney's Wonderful World of Color in *Disney's California Adventure* Park. The show uses music, water screens, digital projection technology, and dazzling lighting effects to celebrate the colorful culture of Disney.

The Streamline Moderne façade of the late
lamented Wurdeman and Becket-designed
Los Angeles landmark, the Pan-Pacific
Auditorium (1935–1989), has been re-created
as the re-imagined entrance to a newly
renovated *Disney's California Adventure* Park.

A specially designed terraced viewing area will enable 9,000 guests to view the Walt Disney's Wonderful World of Color nighttime spectacular on Paradise Bay.

◀◀ The 12-acre *Cars Land* Area includes *Radiator Springs Racers*, a real E-ticket attraction using the latest test track technology and featuring Lightning McQueen racing through switchbacks, tunnels, bridges, and banked turns.

"You can dream, create, design, and build the most wonderful place in the world, but it takes people to make the dream a reality."
—*Walt Disney*

IT TAKES PEOPLE

Excerpt from *The Magic Begins With Me*, 2005

"No one knows better than I . . . what an important role our Cast Members, across the decades and now the world, have played in our success. In creating the magic for our Guests every day, there are few 'starring roles.' But as a nearly 20-year Cast Member myself, I know, as all of you do, that being a Disney Cast Member is one of the most satisfying jobs there is.

"Being a representative of the greatest and most beloved cultural entity of the past century—whether in a front line or a backstage role—is both a great responsibility and an enormous joy. We know that what we do impacts people in a truly tangible and authentic way.

"At Disney we create an encompassing sense of occasion—so much so that for our Guests, their Disney experience becomes part of their personal culture, the collective memory of their family and friends. It is something they treasure, praise, celebrate, and pass on to others.

"But perhaps the most important reason for our success is the ability to involve our Guests in a story—one in which they participate."

—*Jay Rasulo, former Chairman,*
Walt Disney Parks & Resorts, July 17, 2005

More than just workers, *Disneyland* Resort employees are "Cast Members" with a role to play in the "show," part of an encompassing entertainment experience where visitors are both Guest and audience.

◄◄ Even in sunny Southern California, the holiday season calls for spectacular snowfall, even if it is courtesy of a little Disney magic—and the hard work of those industrious elves at Walt Disney Imagineering.

CHRONOLOGY OF MAJOR ATTRACTION
OPENINGS AT DISNEYLAND

1955–1965

King Arthur Carrousel (7/17/55)

Peter Pan's Flight Attraction (7/17/55)

Mad Tea Party Attraction (7/17/55)

Mr. Toad's Wild Ride Attraction (7/17/55)

Canal Boats of the World (7/17/55)

Snow White's Adventures (7/17/55)

Autopia (Tomorrowland Area) (7/17/55)

Space Station X–1 (7/17/55)

Santa Fe and *Disneyland* Railroad (7/17/55)

Circarama, U.S.A. (7/17/55)

Horse-drawn Streetcars (7/17/55)

Fire Wagon (7/17/55)

Main Street Cinema (7/17/55)

Surreys (7/17/55)

Jungle Cruise Attraction (7/17/55)

Stage Coach (7/17/55)

Pack Mules (7/17/55)

Mark Twain Riverboat Attraction (7/17/55)

Penny Arcade (7/17/55)

Golden Horseshoe Revue
   (7/17/55)

Rocket to the Moon (7/22/55)

Main Street Shooting Gallery (7/24/55)

Phantom Boats (7/30/55)

Casey Jr. Circus Train (7/31/55)

Indian Village (7/55)

20,000 Leagues Under the Sea Exhibit
   (8/5/55)

Dumbo The Flying Elephant Attraction
   (8/16/55)

Conestoga Wagons (8/16/55)

Mickey Mouse Club Theater (8/27/55)

Disneyland Hotel (10/55)

Mickey Mouse Club Circus (11/24/55)

Mike Fink Keel Boats (12/25/55)

Astro-Jets (3/24/56)

Horseless Carriage (5/12/56)

Storybook Land Canal Boats (6/16/56)

Tom Sawyer Island (6/16/56)

Skyway to *Tomorrowland* Area (6/23/56)

Skyway to *Fantasyland* Area (6/23/56)

Rainbow Ridge Pack Mules (6/26/56)

Rainbow Mountain Stage Coaches (6/26/56)

Rainbow Caverns Mine Train (7/2/56)

Indian War Canoes (7/4/56)

Junior Autopia (7/23/56)

Omnibus (8/24/56)

Midget Autopia (4/23/57)

Sleeping Beauty Castle [interior] (4/29/57)

Viewliner (6/26/57)

Motor Boat Cruise (6/57 – 01/11/93)

Indian Village Rafts (7/1/57)

Frontierland Shooting Gallery (7/12/57)

Santa Fe & *Disneyland* Railroad, featuring
   the Grand Canyon Diorama (3/1/58)

Alice in Wonderland (6/14/58)

Columbia (6/14/58); below decks, 2/22/64

Fire Truck (8/16/58)

Fantasyland Autopia (1/1/59)

Submarine Voyage (6/6/59)

Matterhorn Bobsleds Attraction (6/14/59)

Disneyland Monorail (6/14/59)

Electric Cars (4/11/60)

Art of Animation (5/28/60)

Mine Train Through
   Nature's Wonderland (5/28/60)

Pack Mules Through
   Nature's Wonderland (6/10/60)

Flying Saucers (8/6/61)

Babes in Toyland Exhibit (12/17/61)

Safari Shooting Gallery (6/15/62)

Swiss Family Treehouse (11/18/62)

Enchanted Tiki Room (6/23/63)

Mickey Mouse Club Headquarters (6/63)

1965–1975

Great Moments with Mr. Lincoln (7/18/65)

it's a small world Attraction (5/28/66)

Santa Fe and *Disneyland* Railroad,
    featuring Grand Canyon Diorama &
    Primeval World (7/1/66)

America the Beautiful (6/25/67)

Pirates of the Caribbean Attraction (3/18/67)

General Electric Carousel of Progress
    (7/2/67)

PeopleMover (7/2/67)

Rocket Jets (7/2/67)

Flight to the Moon (7/67)

Adventure Thru Inner Space (8/12/67)

Haunted Mansion Attraction (8/9/69)

Davy Crockett's Explorer Canoes (5/19/71)

Country Bear Jamboree Show (3/24/72)

Teddi Barra's Swingin' Arcade (3/24/72)

Walt Disney Story (4/8/73)

Disneyland Showcase (4/73)

America Sings (6/29/74)

1975–1985

Mission to Mars (3/21/75)

Walt Disney Story featuring Great
    Moments with Mr. Lincoln (6/12/75)

Space Mountain Attraction (5/4/77)

Starcade (5/4/77)

Sleeping Beauty Castle (11/5/77)

Big Thunder Mountain Railroad Attraction
    (9/2/79)

Pinocchio's Daring Journey (5/25/83)

Peter Pan's Flight Attraction (redesigned
    5/25/83)

Mr. Toad's Wild Ride Attraction
    (redesigned 5/25/83)

Dumbo The Flying Elephant Attraction
    (redesigned 5/25/83)

Snow White's Scary Adventures Attraction
    (redesigned 5/25/83)

Alice in Wonderland (redesigned 4/13/84)

World Premiere Circle-Vision–
    American Journeys (7/4/84)

1985–1995

Big Thunder/Frontierland
    Shooting Arcade (3/85)

Videopolis (6/22/85)

Big Thunder Ranch (6/27/86)

Captain EO (9/18/86)

Star Tours Attraction (1/9/87)

Splash Mountain Attraction (7/17/89)

Toontown Railroad Station (11/25/92)

Mickey's House and Meet Mickey (1/24/93)

Minnie's House (1/24/93)

Goofy's Bounce House (1/24/93)

"Miss Daisy," Donald's Boat (1/24/93)

Chip 'n' Dale's Treehouse and
    Acorn Ball Crawl (1/24/93)

Gadget's Go-Coaster (1/24/93)

Jolly Trolley (1/24/93)

Roger Rabbit's Car Toon Spin (1/26/94)

1995–2005

Indiana Jones™ Adventure and the Temple
    of the Forbidden Eye (3/3/95)

Festival of Foods (6/21/96)

Aladdin and Jasmine's Storytale
    Adventures (Spring, 1997)

Astro Orbitor Attraction (5/22/98)

Honey, I Shrunk the Audience (5/22/98)

Rocket Rods (5/22/98)

Cosmic Waves (6/22/98)

Innoventions Entertainment Facility (7/3/98)

Radio Disney (3/1/99)

Tarzan's Treehouse™ (6/23/99)

Disney's Paradise Pier Hotel (12/00)

Disney's Grand Californian Hotel
& Spa (1/2/01)

Downtown Disney District (1/12/01)

Disney's California Adventure Park (2/8/01)

Soarin' Over California Attraction (2/8/01)

Grizzly River Run (2/8/01)

Redwood Creek Challenge Trail (2/8/01)

Golden Dreams (2/8/01)

Golden Vine Winery (2/8/01)

Seasons of the Vine (2/8/01)

Mission Tortilla Factory (2/8/01)

The Bakery Tour (2/8/01)

Sun Wheel (2/8/01)

California Screamin' Attraction (2/8/01)

Maliboomer (2/8/01)

Mulholland Madness (2/8/01)

Orange Stinger (2/8/01)

Golden Zephyr (2/8/01)

King Triton's Carousel (2/8/01)

Jumpin' Jellyfish (2/8/01)

S.S. rustworthy (2/8/01)

Games of the Boardwalk
(2/8/01, reopened 04/7/09)

Superstar Limo (2/8/01)

Muppet*Vision 3D (2/8/01)

Disney Animation (2/8/01)

Animation Academy (2/8/01)

Character Closeup (2/8/01)

Sorcerer's Workshop (2/8/01)

The Hollywood Backlot Stage (2/8/01)

It's Tough to be a Bug! Attraction (2/8/01)

Bountiful Valley Farm (2/8/01)

Who Wants To Be A Millionaire–
Play It! (9/14/01)

Flik's Fun Fair (10/7/02)

Flik's Flyers (10/7/02)

Francis' Ladybug Boogie (10/7/02)

Heimlich's Chew Chew Train (10/7/02)

Princess Dot Puddle Park (10/7/02)

Tuck and Roll's Drive'Em Buggies (10/7/02)

Disney's Aladdin—A Musical

Spectacular (1/16/03)

Playhouse Disney–Live on Stage! Attraction
(4/11/03)

The Many Adventures of Winnie the Pooh
Attraction (4/11/03)

The Twilight Zone Tower of Terror™
Attraction (5/5/04)

2005–Present

Buzz Lightyear Astro Blasters
Attraction (5/5/05)

Turtle Talk with Crush Attraction (7/15/05)

Monsters, Inc. Mike & Sulley
to the Rescue! Attraction (1/23/06)

Finding Nemo Submarine Voyage
(6/11/07)

Walt Disney Imagineering Blue Sky
Cellar (10/20/08)

Toy Story Midway Mania Attraction
(06/17/08)

INDEX

END SHEETS: *The*
legendary drawing
created by Herb
Ryman and Walt
Disney over a week-
end in September
1953 presented the
Disneyland Park
concept in a way that
even bankers could
understand.